Bitna

Under the Sky of Seoul

Bitna: Under the Sky of Seoul

Published in 2017 by Seoul Selection U.S.A., Inc.
4199 Campus Drive, Suite 550, Irvine, CA 92612
Phone: 949-509-6584 / Seoul office: 82-2-734-9567
Fax: 949-509-6599 / Seoul office: 82-2-734-9562
Email: hankinseoul@gmail.com

ISBN: 978-1-62412-107-4 52400
Library of Congress Control Number: 2017963357

Printed in the Republic of Korea

Musical score on p. 83 courtesy of the Korea Music Copyright Association

J. M. G. Le Clézio

Translated by Brother Anthony of Taizé

Bitna

Under the Sky of Seoul

Seoul Selection

One day or other we'll meet again under the sky of Seoul.

I am grateful to Brother Anthony of Taizé
for his translation and his work in perfecting my novel.

My name is Bitna. I am nearly eighteen years old. I cannot lie, because I have light-colored eyes and it would show immediately. My hair is also light-colored. Some people think it's been bleached with peroxide, but that's the way I was born, with maize-hued hair, because my grandmother suffered from malnutrition, as did my mother after her. I was born down in the south, in the province of Jeolla-do, in a family of fishermen. My parents are not rich, but when I finished my secondary schooling, they wanted to give me the best education, and for that they wanted a top-ranking SKY university, and took out a loan. For my lodgings, I had no problems at first, because my aunt (my father's elder sister) agreed to let me stay in her tiny apartment in the Hongdae neighborhood, right next to Hongik University, where I shared a room with her daughter, named Baekhwa.

I give these details because it's this situation and this neighborhood that were the origin of my later adventures and perfected my education as much as the lessons of my professors. For in that little room I discovered just how much wickedness, jealousy, cowardice, and laziness a person can conceal.

Baekhwa was a few years younger than I was, and I quickly realized that I had been invited to live in the house so that I could take care of her. In the beginning, it was simple requests: "Bitna, you're so reasonable, couldn't you make sure your cousin does her homework" (or tidies her room, or helps with the housework, or says her prayers, or washes her underwear). But gradually the suggestions became more insistent recommendations ("After all, you have to set an example, you know") and finally straight orders: "Bitna! What did I tell you? Go get your cousin, and prepare lunch for her!"

This situation quickly became intolerable. Baekhwa did exactly as she pleased, and her name, meaning "White Flower," did not suit her at all. At the age of fourteen, the only thing that interested her was her own person. She spent hours examining her reflection in a little magnifying mirror, ready to deal with any skin imperfections, redness, or pimples, which she pressed with cotton swabs to extract the pus and then dabbed at with alcohol wipes, before hiding the scars under a layer of concealer covered with foundation. She was a real expert in cosmetic medicine.

It was a battle at every moment, with my long diatribes telling her what she had to do invariably ending in shouts and tears, or fits of anger, when Baekhwa threw everything she could find at my head, or sometimes out of the window—plates, glasses, even knives—and I dared not look outside to see if anyone had been killed. Then I had to clear up the wreckage, and also endure the reproaches of my aunt: "You're so ungrateful. After all that we've done for you, all that we're doing to help you in life. If it wasn't for me, you'd be begging in the street. Or you could go back home to your family down in Jeolla-do, scaling and gutting fish in the marketplace." What could I say to that?

It was at that time that I began to roam about the city. The courses at the university only take up part of my time. I spend the rest walking the streets, or undertake long journeys by bus and subway. At first, I went out to forget about my family problems, the filthiness of the room I shared with my cousin, and my aunt's incessant reproaches. The moment I leave the apartment, slamming the metal door and descending the steep steps leading to the street, I feel freed of a burden. I breathe more freely. I have energy in my legs, and I am smiling.

The street is my adventure playground. In my little town down in Jeolla-do nothing much happens. The center is just one or two streets, with a few shops, mainly food stores, and a few restaurants; life stops at five in the evening, and the busiest moment of the day is early in the morning when tractors arrive pulling carts filled with cabbages and onions. We live to the rhythm of the festivals, three times a year—the Lunar New Year, the spring festival when we repair the family graves, and the autumn festival of Chuseok. When I arrived in Seoul, I felt as if I had entered a new world. The various neighborhoods are surrounded by wide avenues, along which flows an endless stream of cars and buses, speeding off in all directions. On the pavements the crowd is so compact that I learned to walk without banging into the people coming from the opposite direction, which means, given my size (I measure 1.56 meters and I weigh 43 kilograms), jumping to one side and sometimes even stepping off the sidewalk. At first, I would accompany my aunt in her shopping, or my cousin. They had an assurance that impressed me. They never stepped off the sidewalk, but on the contrary, pressed together to form a compact block and advanced without looking to either side. It was the technique of the tank. I stayed cautiously behind them, following in their wake. I looked every person straight in the eye, and that is not done. At the beginning, I even greeted pedestrians in the street, especially the elderly, until my aunt scolded me: "Bitna, why are you smiling at everyone? You want to be taken for a nutcase?" Baekhwa laughed at me: "She's a country girl, she doesn't know the city!"

It was during this first year that I got into the habit of watching people without their realizing it. It's not always easy. You have to find a good observation post, not too far away, but not too close either. In the subway, there are reflections in the windows, but they're not always very clear, and people spot you fast enough when they turn toward the windows and meet your reflection. Buses are better, because it's daylight and you can make your observations through the windows. Either people are in cars, and you look down on them because the bus is higher, or when the bus stops, then moves slowly along, you have time to see the people on the sidewalk well and imagine all sorts of things about them. Where they come from, what they do in life, their worries, their emotional problems, their money problems, or what they have gone through, their memories, their families, their sorrows.

I always had a little notebook, and I noted everything I saw, with a quick description of the people:

A lady of about fifty. Dressed in a slightly threadbare black coat, with low shoes, carrying a handbag in imitation leather with two golden buckles. She has curled gray hair and wrinkles on each side of her mouth. Lives in Gangnam, in an apartment block. Divorced. Her apartment is very small. She would like to have a dog, but the rules forbid it. Her name is Mrs. Na Misuk. She used to work in a bank, behind a window, counting banknotes, making transfers. Then she resigned before reaching retirement age. She once thought of committing suicide, but she did not have the courage.

The bus began to move again, and the woman met my eyes. She looked surprised, and looked away. A moment later, as the bus was moving along slowly, I looked back, and she smiled at me.

A young woman, alone at the edge of the sidewalk, where there is no bus stop; she seems to be waiting for someone. Her boyfriend is coming to fetch her by car, but he is already very late. She has an impatient wrinkle between her eyebrows. She is thinking that she ought to leave, but her feet are riveted to the ground, she cannot move. It's like a bad dream . . . I want to call her Miss Ko Eunji, I think that name suits her. Maybe tomorrow if I take the same bus, No. 6712, she will still be in the same place. Her boyfriend has decided to break up with her. He no longer answers the phone. And she dares not go to his place because he is married.

An old woman, she must come from the south. I can see it in her face, blackened by the sun. Her back is bent from working in the fields. She has come up to accompany her daughter and her granddaughter to the hospital. She is afraid she will arrive late at the rendezvous, so she rushes toward the bus, then draws back. Her eyes are very small. She has crow's feet on her cheeks, a mole on the ridge of her nose. Her daughter is called Yunjin, married for three years now with a civil servant, with a little girl named Yungyeong. Yunjin chose her daughter a name similar to her own, although that is usually only done between sisters, but she has also given her a Christian name, Maria, because her husband is a Christian.

I noted the names, the places, as if I would see those people again, but I knew I never would. The city was so big, we could walk a million days without meeting the same person twice, despite the saying: "One day or other we'll meet again under the sky of Seoul."

Then I found the best place to learn about people. It was in the big bookstore in Jongno. When I finished my classes, I took the subway and went to the basement store with all of its books. For me, it was incredible, to have access to so many, because at home in Jeolla-do there was no money to buy books. I only had school textbooks that were very worn, soiled, and greasy, with pages scribbled on by the generations of schoolchildren who had held them. So after I discovered this world, I could not do without it. Every day, when I finished class, I went to the bookstore and settled myself in a corner to look at the books. From the start, I especially liked the shelves of foreign books. I took down volumes at random and began to read them. I read Dickens's novels. There was one I liked very much, *The Cricket on the Hearth*. When I began to read, everything around me disappeared. I heard the music of the great pot over the fire, and the song of the cricket whistling in the ashes somewhere, without anyone seeing it, and I imagined that

I was in that great room by the fire, and that I was listening to the voice of Charles Dickens telling this story for me alone, in the English language. Other authors I read were Mazo de la Roche, *Building of Jalna*, or Margaret Mitchell, *Gone with the Wind*, and later I found a collection of tales by Edgar Allan Poe, where I read *The Black Cat* and *The Oval Portrait*. The words fascinated me. I forgot all about time. I also read books in French, because two years earlier I had decided I was going to learn that language, so gentle and musical. There were only a few books in French, including the poems of Jacques Prévert, which I was very fond of.

Once, while I was reading, a young man came and stood close to me, watching me, and his gaze was so insistent that I had to tear my eyes away from the book.

"Excuse me," he said, "but the store will close in five minutes."

I was confused and blushed. I tried to explain myself: "I can't decide which book to buy, I'm sorry."

He bowed politely, as if it did not matter. "No, no, you don't need to decide right away, you can come back tomorrow."

He was not very tall. He had pretty, black, almond-shaped eyes and a delicate nose; I thought I might include him, one day, among my favorite characters. I invented a name for him right away. I called him Mr. Pak.

It was in that bookstore that I really started to learn about people. The bus, the subway, or the sidewalk were not good places, because people moved too much, walked fast, ran away. Or, on the contrary, they stopped, and it was I who became the object of observation. And that was the most terrible thing, because what I wanted was to be invisible, to see without being seen.

Then, one day, something changed in my life. As I was putting a book I had skimmed through back on the shelf, Mr. Pak came to talk to me.

"Come with me," he said, "I have something to show you."

I didn't know what he wanted, but I followed him obediently. Perhaps I imagined for a moment that he was going to offer me a job in the bookstore, and that was my dream, because I really liked reading books, and I urgently needed some money. My aunt kept telling me, at the least occasion, "You're costing us so much; we'll have to find a way to pay for your studies and lodging." Even worse, my cousin knew. She purposely tried to upset everything in the room, for the pleasure of seeing me tidy up after her.

Mr. Pak opened the drawer of his desk and handed me a letter. It was typed, and it said:

My name is Kim Seri, but I go by Salome. I can no longer leave my house because of my illness. I am waiting for someone to come and tell me about the world. I like stories. I am serious about this. In exchange for your stories I will pay you a good salary.

There was a phone number.

Mr. Pak handed me the letter and I took it mechanically, folded it, and put it in my bag with my books and my English textbooks. I didn't think about it until I came across it a few days later. I picked up the phone and called Salome.

The first story I told Salome
April 2016

In the spring, when the buds begin to open and the wind blows, longing for flowers, Mr. Cho Hansu carries the cages holding his pigeons up onto the roof. Mr. Cho has the right to do that because he's the janitor, and the only one with the key. The building is a large apartment block from the 1980s, part of a multi-block complex called, goodness knows why, "Good Luck!" (complete with an exclamation mark), maybe because it's so far from any hope of fortune or happiness. It is devoid of any style, with thousands of identical windows and hundreds of small glazed balconies where tenants hang their washing to dry in the pale sunshine that passes through. The number 19 is painted in black on the side wall of Mr. Cho's building. There are eighteen others, all similar, but number 19 is the best, at the top of the hill above Yongsan. From the roof, on the twentieth floor, Mr. Cho can look out across the city, its great cement office blocks emerging from the mist.

In the spring, the sun is already hot, and the

pigeons in their cages are excited by the warm wind, by the odors that rise from the branches of the pine trees all around. They coo and jostle. They stretch their necks to try to see outside. They forget about the wire netting nailed to the sides of the cages. Some people remark at the sight, "Pigeons are the stupidest creatures in all of nature!" They point out that the birds are trying to escape through holes so small that only half of their beaks fit. "Just look at the size of their brains," they say. Mr. Cho has tried once or twice to contradict them: "But they fly. Can you imagine what it is to fly? Isn't that better than driving a car or filling in a sudoku?" Everyone, including neighbors, other residents, and even caretakers of the other buildings, know about Mr. Cho's obsession with his pigeons.

During the winter, the pigeons and Mr. Cho all sink into a sort of idle lethargy. Mr. Cho has an agreement with the building administrator, to act as janitor of the building but without receiving any salary. In exchange, he's allowed to keep his homing pigeons with him and take them up onto the wide, flat roof to get some air. "But you must be careful that the birds don't make a mess, and you must not take them up in the elevator!" Mr. Cho agrees. Of course, the administrator is doing him a favor, because Mr. Cho was a former policeman, and it's always useful to have a policeman around. Mr. Cho has been the janitor of block 19 for five years, but before that he lived in the countryside in Ganghwado Island, in a village close to North Korea. He grew up in that village. His mother crossed through the fighting carrying him on her back and headed southward. She finally settled in Ganghwado Island, growing onions and potatoes, first as a worker, then after remarrying with the owner of the farm. When Mr. Cho was growing up, there was no longer war, but neither was there peace. There were soldiers everywhere, the roads were only used by tanks and trucks, and there was an American base nearby.

All Mr. Cho knows about the home of his mother, his grandparents, and his father is the name, Gaeseong. His grandfather, about whom his mother sometimes told him, was a very handsome man, very brown-skinned, with a lot of hair, a singer of *pansori*. He was also the owner of a pear plantation through his wife. A rich man, his mother had said, authoritarian but generous.

"What happened to him after the war?"

"Oh, he's been dead for a long time, and now there's no one who remembers him on this side of the border."

Except Mr. Cho, because he remembers everything his mother told him. When she died, she carried away all those memories with her. Mr. Cho's love of pigeons is something he owes to his mother. When she crossed the combat zone, she took with her a couple of homing pigeons her father had brought up. With the young Mr. Cho on her back, she carried the birds in a small bag pierced with holes so that they could breathe. She took them so that one day they might fly back to their native land, bringing news to her family on the other side. But time passed and Mr. Cho's mother did not have the heart to send the pigeons back, so they went on living on this side of the frontier, grew old, and died. But in the meantime, they had many children, and these are the pigeons that Mr. Cho has brought up, with the thought that perhaps one day they might accomplish their intended mission. He hasn't spoken of it to anybody, though, for who would believe that birds might retain the memory of their country of origin up to the third or fourth generation?

It's morning. There is no better time for the pigeons. Mr. Cho has carried up five cages, one after another. In each cage are two pairs of pigeons, separated by a strong cardboard partition. Each couple share a name, a sort of surname, and each individual bird has a first name. This may seem meaningless. Mrs. Li, Mr. Cho's neighbor, remarked to him one day, "Why do you give names to those birds? Do pigeons know their names? They aren't dogs, after all!"

Mr. Cho looked at her reproachfully. "But they know their names, madam. They're much smarter than your dog, if you want my opinion."

Mrs. Li could not accept that. She liked contradicting people, and she was happy that for once Mr. Cho had responded to her.

"That's the most ridiculous thing I've heard in a long time," she said. "What do your pigeons have on my dog?"

"They fly, madam," said Mr. Cho.

The reply was categorical, and it left Mrs. Li stumped. Later, she thought, "Why, I should have told him that flying is not a sign of intelligence and if Frog"—this was the name of her dog, because he was small, short-legged, and plumpish, and croaked like a frog rather than a dog—"had wings, he'd be able to fly, too."

So on this spring morning, Mr. Cho carries his five cages all the way up to the roof. He doesn't take the elevator, because as janitor he respects his agreement with the administrator not to bring pigeon cages into the elevator. Otherwise, he might receive a reprimand from the bank that owns the building, reported by a malicious inhabitant claiming to be allergic to bird feathers. That would degenerate into a quarrel, and Mr. Cho doesn't like quarrels.

Mr. Cho arrives on the roof panting, because he has climbed up the twenty floors five times, all the way up to the roof. He calculates this to be about 400 steps each time, which means 2,000 steps for the entire trip. Mr. Cho is no longer young. After thirty years of service in the police, he is long past retirement, and he can feel in his legs and in his lungs that he's no longer twenty, or even thirty-five. So, once up on the roof, he grants himself a little respite, sitting on top of a ventilation shaft, looking out at the landscape of the city as it slowly emerges from the morning mist. In a few moments, he will clearly see Namsan Mountain and the spire of the radio tower, and a little beyond that the great shining serpent of the Hangang River with, a bit further on, the silhouettes of the skyscrapers of Gangnam and the ribbons of the highways. It's a Sunday morning, still early, and the noise of the town is diminished, as if everyone is holding their breath for what is to follow.

And then it is time. The pigeons wait for him with growing impatience. They turn on themselves in the narrow space of the cages, they try to beat their wings, and their pinions emit a whistle that underlines their impatience. Mr. Cho feels this in his own body, like an electric fluid flowing along his limbs and escaping at the tips of his fingers, raising the little hairs on the backs of his hands. He crouches in front of the cages. He speaks to the birds, pronouncing their names slowly, one by one:

Vixen, and you, the male, Finch
Blue, and you, Robin
Rocket, White Arrow
Light, Moon
Fly, Cicada
Traveling Girl, President

Acrobat, Snail
Diamond, Black Dragon
Singer, King
Dancer, Saber

He says their names, his face close to the cages, one by one. Each time, the bird named stops fidgeting, turns its head backward, and looks up with its yellow eyes. And Mr. Cho feels as if he has received a confidence, a word of thanks and also a promise. A promise of what? He can't say, but that's how it feels, something uniting itself with him, giving him a memory of the past, something like a dream that continues on again after days of sleep.

It is time. Mr. Cho opens a long tin box, rather like a schoolboy's pencil case. Inside are a series of messages that he has prepared, written by hand very neatly on fine, almost translucent rice paper. He imagined them for a long time before writing them. He didn't want to write just anything. He didn't simply want to enjoy himself, even though his daughter Sumi teased him, saying, "So, Dad, are you writing to your sweetheart?" Or "Don't forget to include your phone number!" She, of course, doesn't believe in it. It wasn't part of her generation, nor even of the generation of the elderly folk who live in the same building. They live in their time. They make fun of Mr. Cho's imaginings. They have the Internet, they write on their mobile phones, on their screens, using text messaging. It has been a long time since they have written any letters by hand. Yet Sumi, only a few years ago, still liked to write letters. Mr. Cho remembers that she even composed small poems for him to roll like cigarettes and put in the capsules hanging from the legs of the pigeons. And then she lost interest. When they moved into this building, in the center of this very large city, she stopped believing in the pigeons and their messages, and became like everyone else.

It's time. Mr. Cho opens the cage holding Black Dragon. He picks the bird up gently. He holds it in his cupped hands. He feels the heart beating very quickly in its chest, the gentle warmth of its belly, and its cold feet. With the tips of his thumbs, he caresses the bird, brings it up to his face, and blows on its head, and on the tip of its beak. The pigeon blinks its eyes, then opens them, and its pupils dilate, because it has realized that it is time to do what it does best, to fly.

The wind rises, a mixture of sweetness and bitterness. Mr. Cho knows this moment of the year, the one he prefers, the time of what people call "the wind that envies the flowers in their blooming"—the memory of snow mixed with the perfume of the plum blossom opening down in the valley. No plum trees are here, though, only the plants in pots that several of the inhabitants of Good Luck! cultivate in their spare moments. Along with a few flowerless magnolias down below, lined up along the side of the building.

Black Dragon struggles in his master's hands. Under the downy feathers Mr. Cho feels the bird's little heart racing, like a tiny bell. He whispers to him, softly, words that encourage, not phrases, just carefully chosen words. Sweet words, round words, light words. "Wind," "spirit," "light," "wing," "love," "return," "grass," "snow." For Black Dragon, he only needs one word: "hope." And for his companion, Diamond, Mr. Cho chooses "desire," because it also means "wind." Black Dragon listens. The pupils in his yellow eyes grow round, and at the back of his throat Mr. Cho can hear small pebbles rolling, the words of his language, the language of his throat alone. Because in fact, the whole of the bird's body wants to speak, the pinions, the wings, the feathers of its tail, to pierce the air and speak by diving into the air's currents. Slowly, Mr. Cho approaches the edge of the roof and stretches out his arms as if offering the bird to the sky. *Vouff!* Black Dragon takes flight. At first, he drops toward the street, then suddenly gains control, soaring upward, and begins his flight over the buildings, in the direction of the rising sun.

In her cage, Diamond is impatient. She has heard the sound of wings. She knows it's her turn now, and she calls out. When Mr. Cho takes her in his hands, she pecks at him, as if to say, "Let go of me, you idiot. My lover is already up in the sky, so let me go join him!" Mr. Cho doesn't have to go to the edge of the roof. He opens his hands and Diamond leaps up. She is lighter than the male. She goes straight up into the sky, flies in an arc above the avenue, and in a few moments, she has vanished into the light. Mr. Cho cannot follow her with his eyes. His eyes are weak, and the intensity of the sun makes him cry.

So Mr. Cho begins his long wait. He knows that it might last hours, sometimes even until night. He sits on the roof next to the cages, closes his eyes, and tries to imagine what Black Dragon and Diamond are seeing above the city. The high glassed apartment blocks, standing like crystal cliffs, highways like ribbons, and then the great river. The energy accumulated in their wings during weeks of confinement would have turned into an electric force; their wings would beat at full speed, the wind currents would push them upwards, then the chilly patches above the river would make them drop. Black Dragon would lead the way as far as the river, then Diamond, following the bank as far as the bridge, towards the island. There are other birds in the sky, lower down, sea birds, gulls, and near the island, groups of ducks. The pigeons do not stop. They circle above the water, the surface shimmers and shivers, the tufts of grass and reeds bend in the wind. On the great bridge, the cars are stopped by the morning traffic jam, a roaring of horns, or perhaps the cries of the ducks, or the whistle of the train slowly crossing the river. To keep him company while he waits, Mr. Cho has brought with him one of his oldest boarders, a pigeon that his mother knew, perhaps even a son of the original pair. His name is Jojongsa, which means "pilot," because he once flew high like a plane. But now he is blind, and paralyzed by arthritis, so that he simply stays in his master's hands without moving, breathing the wind and feeling the sun caressing his feathers.

Salome was clapping. Her eyes were shining. She tried to gesture, but she lost control of her left hand, and instead of touching her forehead, it struck her nose, and she made a grotesque grimace.

"You want to rest a bit now, surely?" I said.

Salome was tall and thin, but because of her illness she was huddled up in her wheelchair. She had a tartan blanket over her slender legs, so that nobody would see that she was wearing diapers. She knew how to laugh about it, nonetheless. She had once said, "It's so that no one can see that my legs are trembling, I don't want to lose my happiness!" Indeed, I knew the saying, too, and I liked that she had the courage to make fun of herself. I insisted.

"You must be tired?"

"No, everything's fine," she said. Yet it seemed not in her character to be too easily content. "I like your story. It makes me feel I can fly like Mr. Cho's pigeons above the city, I feel so light!" She sniggered briefly, sarcastically. "But I want to know the names!"

I did not understand. "Names, what names?"

She made a gesture of impatience. "The names of the places they fly to, your pigeons. Tell me the names!"

So I told her names of various places, all the places I knew in this city, and also places that didn't exist, that

I had never seen, that I had only seen in my dreams.

Black Dragon and Diamond flew over the apartment blocks, as far as the Hangang River, then they passed over Yeouido, the great white building of the National Assembly, and the parks where little old folk take their grandchildren walking on Sunday afternoons. Then they swerved to one side, and passed over the bridge known as Dangsan Railway Bridge, with millions of cars following behind each other like insects on Olympic Expressway below it. They did not stop there. They passed over the island with the ducks, then they flew back, still following the river, and Cheonggyecheon Stream. They went as far as Myeong-dong, above Savoy Hotel, where there are plenty of small streets and dark alleys, and they passed above the great mountain, maybe because Diamond longed to stop for a moment in the pines on the mountain. She liked so much the smell of their needles, and she hoped that one day Black Dragon might decide to build a nest there, but he beat his wings and made a long sweep toward Jongno, and the tower with the Kyobo Book

Centre. Together they flew as far as Insa-dong, then on to Changgyeonggung Palace, gliding next above the Secret Garden of Changdeok-gung Palace, where the water of the small lakes sparkled in the sun and there was the smell of trees and flowers. The wind descending from the mountains pushed them back, and soon they were above Dongdaemun Gate. They continued on past Samcheong-dong, and Mr. Cho, on the dusty roof of his building, could imagine what they saw—the traditional roofs, some with varnished tiles that shone, the gardens, the square inner courtyards. Then, the pigeons began their return, flying near Gyeongbokgung Palace, and on above the railway station. They dropped lower, in the direction of the sun. It was already the end of the day, and they were tired from having flown so far. They made another half-circle around the Samsung office building, and then the wind of the river, or the solar wind, pushed them back toward the tall silhouette against Yongsan, back to the flat roof where Mr. Cho was waiting.

Salome's face was feverish. While I said the names

she closed her eyes, and she glided through the air with the pair of pigeons. She went from one street to the other. She felt the breeze off the river and heard the mingled noises of cars, trucks, buses, and also the metallic screech of a train sliding along its rails near Sinchon Station.

I invented names: Songsi, Myeongju, Cheonggang, Byeolhae, Palanggaebi, Dokhae, Hongno . . .

They did not mean anything, but Salome believed in them. Her hands, very white, were gripping the arms of her chair, as if it had taken off and was gliding along under the clouds. Then Salome slipped down a bit against the back of the chair. Her closed eyes tinged her white eyelids with blue, and she fell asleep. Gently, without making any noise, I rose and took the envelope containing the 50,000 won notes. My name was written on it in large, irregular letters:

빛나

I pushed open the studio door and went out into the street.

It was around this time that things began to go downhill at home. There were more and more scenes, in part at least because my dear little cousin, that delightful Baekhwa, had started going out in the evenings, hanging out with boys, and generally becoming a degenerate young woman.

"With your experience of life," my aunt would say, addressing me—I wondered what experience she meant—"you should tell her to behave herself. She's doing nothing at school. She says she doesn't want to go on, that it's pointless."

You couldn't say I hadn't tried. After all, I felt a bit sorry for her. She'd always been the family's spoiled brat, and she knew nothing about life. I gave her a lecture one afternoon. I waited for her to get out of school and we went to a Lavazza coffee place in Hongdae. She took a seat outside so she could smoke.

"Maybe you're too young to be smoking?" I said.

"Because you don't smoke?"

"I didn't when I was your age."

"And what difference does that make now?"

I let it drop. After all, whether she smoked in public or in secret was none of my business.

"You can do as you like, but you're not trying in class."

"How would you know that?"

"Look, I've seen your report cards. You're absent all the time, and your grades are a disaster."

"So what do my grades have to do with you?"

Things suddenly got heated. She was leaning toward me. I could see her dilated pupils, and the little veins on her forehead were swollen in anger.

"You know, you're nothing, just a kid from the backwoods, and now, because you're at university, you reckon you're superior to everybody else. Why don't you go back to Jeolla-do and catch squid?"

I suddenly found her ugly and vulgar. As I listened to her insults, I couldn't help thinking how similar she was to my aunt, with the same broad face, receding chin, and low forehead, only twenty years apart. And I couldn't help thinking that her remark about the squid was probably something she'd heard from my aunt, who must have said the same kind of things behind my back.

I came to a decision. Using the money I received from Salome, I rented a tiny room in another part of town, on the hill above Sinchon. The advantage was that the room had a separate entrance, so there was no need for me to see the owner. It was only a semi-basement room with an old washbasin and toilet hidden by a plastic curtain. It was rather damp and dark, but it was all mine. I no longer had to listen to my cousin's moaning or my aunt's reproaches, to say nothing of my uncle's snoring. I went to my classes, bought little things to eat, Coke, cigarettes. I was the happiest girl in the world. I had never imagined how great it was to be alone, completely alone, with no need to see anyone. As for those women who complain that they have no friends, that they're lonely—well, I can't understand them. They don't realize how lucky they are. I didn't even need a boyfriend. All the boys I met seemed to be inflated idiots, real little kings, spoiled by their mothers, by their girlfriends, by their older sisters, their teachers. They were only interested in themselves. They spent most of the time doing their hair, applying perfumed skin lotion, then checking their hair using the camera on their phones. Those who came up to me and tried spinning their yarns, I soon got rid of. All it took was a little critical remark and they soon lost heart: "Oh, you and your acne!" or "Has nobody ever told you that you smell?" or "Where on earth did you dig up that jacket? You look like a garage mechanic!" It did the trick. They went off to try their luck some-where else. They reminded me of those crooks who trick people by talking to them about another world, lure them to some isolated place outside the city, and steal all their money.

The only person I wanted to see again was Salome. Not because she had employed me to tell her stories but because of the way she listened to me, as if drinking in my every word, as if all her bottled-up energy was emerging through her eyes. Then she phoned me one morning. I was in class. I saw her number appear on the screen, but I did not call her back. At lunchtime, while I was in the university canteen emptying down a bowl of soup, she phoned again.

"*Moshi-moshi.*" (That was the way she said hello on the phone, in Japanese.) "I need you. I want to hear more of your story. Why haven't you called me?"

"I had work to do at school. I was asked to organize a seminar about translation."

That was the truth, but I had mostly been occupied by my move. I could not talk to her about that, though, since we had decided never to talk about real life, and I really liked that, because I think people tend to chatter too much about little problems that interest only themselves. Salome had significant health problems, but she only mentioned them once, to explain that she could not walk and that nurses came twice a day to change and wash her. Because she wanted me to understand why she could not accompany me to the door. I had never known anyone in such a state. Even my grandmother, before she died, could walk, bent over, as far as outside the door to feed her chickens.

"I'll be waiting for you this afternoon. You will come, won't you?"

I didn't hesitate. "This afternoon, then, at five o'clock."

"Ah, Bitna, you're an angel."

She said this in English, and the next moment I received on my phone a picture of a funny little character with a crown of birds dancing on its head.

I took the bus to her street, near the French high school in the southern part of the city. The sun was shining brightly. I had never realized how pretty her neighborhood was, with small luxurious apartment buildings surrounded by gardens, or modern villas. There were dogs behind the walls, barking fiercely when I passed the gates. There were not many pedestrians in this neighborhood. It was not like Sinchon, where almost everybody walked on foot, some pulling carts loaded with vegetables or wheelbarrows piled with old boxes. In Salome's neighborhood—I had only come once before—even the cars seemed not to be moving. They were parked obediently in the spaces marked on the roadway. In front of the entrance to Salome's building, I thought that I recognized the car belonging to her nurse, a gray Kia, parked along the wall. It was somehow reassuring, but also, like everything else that does not change, scary, and I almost turned back. It was the memory of Salome's voice, her grave voice when she had said, "Later, tell me later, please!" which gave me the courage to ring at the door. The nurse let me in. I took off my sneakers and put on the slippers she held out to me. She did not say anything, especially nothing like "Miss Salome is waiting for you." Such were Salome's instructions, above all to use none of those ordinary phrases. Silence.

The room was lit up by the late afternoon sun, and I was glad I had chosen this time. I would not have liked dark, cold air or the smell of the sickroom. On the contrary, it smelled of the jasmine tea the nurse had prepared for us, which was steaming on the little card table next to Salome. It was like a ritual, although it was only the second time, and I like anything that resembles a ritual. It made me want to begin telling my stories, a bit like an impatience that makes one's hands tremble. It might sound a bit vain, but as I arrived in front of Salome's building I had gotten the feeling that it was my destiny to help her find delight in life. And I liked that. When I crossed the threshold of the house, I still had no idea what story I was going to tell. Whether it would be the rest of Mr. Cho's story, or the story of Miss Kitty, or whether I should invent a story about a murderer. I decided it would be Miss Kitty.

The second story I told Salome

May 2016

Miss Kitty arrived in the beauty salon early one morning, while Mrs. Lim was preparing everything for the customers: the chairs, clean linen, the implements, and the big kettle for green tea. Mrs. Lim's salon was not very big, but everything was well organized to receive women who wanted to get their hair styled, dyed, or curled. The clientele was not very varied, and mainly consisted of women of a certain age. Mrs. Lim knew their surnames and forenames, and even several small secrets, like those that hairdressers and manicurists generally collect. So Miss Kitty's arrival in Mrs. Lim's room was strange, unexpected, and something which might rightly be considered surprising. At that moment, she was a stranger, with no name. It was not until later, after one or two months, that she was given the name Kitty, perhaps after the Japanese character, or because Mrs. Lim had heard someone say it. In any case, her arrival turned the salon topsy-turvy. Mrs. Lim's two employees, Jo-Eun and Yeri, commented on her at length, making assumptions, in a totally illogical and absolutely emotional disorder:

She's very thin, she must have come from the north, from the country. No, it's impossible for her to have come from so far away, I would say that she's city-born. Look, she's not afraid of anything. She came to us directly, as if she knew the neighborhood. She's surely city-born! You're from Yeongwol, you're able to tell the difference? In any case she's not hard up, did you see her fur? That beautiful gray, with not a spot on it, she surely hasn't been rolling about in countryside mud. And she knows this neighborhood well, so she must live in that big building there, next door, the Good Luck! Or maybe she's from the cold noodle restaurant, or from the gambling den where they play cards. From the gambling den? You really are full of nonsense, what would she be doing with all these drunks? I'm not sure, but I think I've seen her before near the Christian church. The pastor there must be taking care of her. It wouldn't surprise me, she looks so pious! Now you're talking nonsense. Why not say she's a Buddhist from Jogyesa Temple, or that temple up on Namsan Mountain, while you're at it? Why else would she be coming here?

This salon is not for chic folks, it's just for the neighborhood *ajumma,* right?

"Chatter, chatter," concluded Ms. Lim. "What gossips you are. Get back to work. There are cloths to be washed, and scissors, and polishers. I'm not paying you to talk nonsense about our visitor, our traveler."

So that's what they called her to start with. She was called the Traveler. It was a name that suited her well.

Do you know me? Do you know my name, and where I live? If you read this message, please write a reply below. Please call ...

This was the kind of message the Traveler began to carry in a little bag hung round her neck—a very small bag of braided straw, more like a purse than a bag. It was Mrs. Lim who first had the idea. Not that she was really interested in the Traveler's origins and misadventures. But her curiosity was piqued by the mystery that surrounded her, by that obscure, almost evil aspect she imagined surrounding her. For Mrs. Lim, there was no such thing as chance, not in the world. Everything had a cause, a meaning, and a finality. The Traveler could not simply have arrived one day in her neighborhood, in her shop at the entrance of the Good Luck! complex, without it signifying a change in the established order, a kind of blurring of wavelengths that would lead to something both unpredictable and disturbing.

"Anyway, she's come from somewhere," she argued in front of her employees. "Or else someone has sent her to us."

"You should ask her yourself," joked a client, a large woman of about fifty who came in regularly to have her hair curled, and whom Mrs. Lim looked down on, because despite being the wife of a pastor of the neighboring church, she was stingy and always took issue with what the salon charged her, especially for the massage of her thick neck, which she demanded at the end of the session as if it were her right.

"That's exactly what I'm going to do, you can be sure," Mrs. Lim replied. And it was on that day that she got the idea of the messages and the little woven straw bag.

For several weeks, the little bag kept its secret. The notes went unanswered. Then, one fine day, when Mrs. Lim no longer expected it, the Traveler came back. She came into the salon without any fear, as if she knew everybody, and as if it was the most natural thing for her to sit down on one of the black imitation-leather armchairs and wait for someone to come and look after her. Mrs. Lim was really excited. She would not let anyone else approach her. She prepared a small snack for her, balls of rice with some fish, and she put the dish in front of her.

"You must be hungry, after all your travels, so eat first, then we can talk a little."

Talk was a big word, because Mrs. Lim did not really expect any conversation. She gave the Traveler time to eat while she prepared to serve her client at the moment, an old lady who was slightly deaf and determined to have her hair dyed blue. Mrs. Lim's other employees also continued to do their jobs, but each of them kept glancing sideways to observe the Traveler's behavior. She ate quietly from the plate, without hurrying.

"She's not hungry," thought Mrs. Lim.

This was sure proof that the Traveler was no ordinary vagabond. She had to have her own house, her habits, someone who took care of her.

This reassured Mrs. Lim, and at the same time increased her curiosity. Why, if all her needs were met, and she had a house and loved ones around her, would she venture into this salon, sit down in a chair, and wait to be served? This thought made her shudder, and she began to imagine that the Traveler was not what she seemed to be, but rather one come from beyond, an incarnation of someone she had once known, back after years of being forgotten, wanting to be recognized. Mrs. Lim hurried to finish preparations for the blue dye, and left her client with the plastic cap fastened around her head before running to the armchair at the end of the room to speak to the Traveler. For her part, the Traveler showed no signs of impatience. After eating the rice balls, she yawned lazily, and now seemed half-asleep on the chair, her head resting against the cushion, her eyes half closed, allowing a little of the yellow of her irises to filter through. Mrs. Lim was in such a hurry that she stretched out her hands toward the Traveler's neck without pausing to wipe them. The Traveler immediately drew back, as if she disliked the pungent odor of the dye.

"Oh, I'm so sorry," said Mrs. Lim. "I know this

smell is not very pleasant. I'll go and wash my hands." Which she did, carefully, using the sink just in front of the chair. Then, as she did not really know how to position herself, she crouched down in front of the chair, so that her face was eye-level with the Traveler's.

"Now, let's see what messages you've brought me."

Delicately, she detached the bag of woven straw from the Traveler's neck and opened it. Her heart leapt when she discovered in the bag a small sheet of paper folded in four—it was not at all like the messages she had left a few days previously. The paper was thin, of a slightly purple color, and bore a few words written in felt-tip, in childish letters.

I live on the fifteenth floor of the apartment block
I have no name, no family
Who am I?

The other employees came running up and surrounded Mrs. Lim, trying to read the words of the message over her shoulder, but Mrs. Lim didn't let them see it. She straightened herself, carefully folded the letter, and slipped it into her apron pocket.

"Well, what does it say?" asked Youn, the youngest.

"Yes, what's the answer?" the others echoed.

Even the blue-haired old lady arrived, her cap still on her head. "What's going on here?"

One of the employees tried to explain. "It's nothing, it's the reply that's arrived."

The old woman grumbled. "All right, all right. I want to have my dye job finished, please."

The Traveler, the object of all this curiosity, did not seem to care. She stretched herself languorously, and laid her delicate little head against an arm of the chair, looking in another direction.

She stayed there the whole morning, and part of the afternoon, dozing in her chair. Then, when closing time came, Mrs. Lim decided to write another letter. The employees left after sweeping the floor and stowing away the instruments. Outside, night was drawing in, the lights were coming on, and you could hear the soft sound of cars bringing residents back to the apartment block after a day of work. An orange seller had stationed himself with his little cart at one corner of the avenue and was announcing his wares through a loudspeaker that crackled.

Ms. Lim finished writing her note. She had thought about it a little, and she thought it was time to give the Traveler a name: *Miss Kitty.*

I am at the hair salon at the entrance of the Good Luck! complex.
If you know Miss Kitty, please reply.
Thank you.

Mrs. Lim put the carefully folded sheet of paper into the little bag, closed the cord around the opening, and paused. Miss Kitty must have been waiting for that, because she immediately got up out of the chair and headed toward the door, took a few steps along the pavement as if hesitating about which direction to take, and disappeared in an instant. Mrs. Lim rushed to the door to observe her, but she had already disappeared behind the bushes adorning the entrance to the apartments. Mrs. Lim felt a kind of little pang in her heart, as if she was never going to see her again, as if it was the last time Miss Kitty would visit the shop. That evening, Mrs. Lim went home to her husband and daughter, but she was careful not to talk to them about what had happened. It was like a secret, and if she talked about it, she thought, she risked losing it, like a fragile dream that fades away as soon as you try to put it into words.

The afternoon was well advanced, and the sun was only shining on the wall at the back of the room, where Salome had hung a board of yellow wood with all her family photos. I did not dare to stop in front of the board, but I had caught a glimpse of the portrait of a lady in a two-piece suit, tall and stern-looking, in front of a photo-studio landscape, with waterfalls and old monuments. I thought to myself that I might one day invent the story of this woman, make her a traveler like Miss Kitty, who lived in Australia a long time ago and died in a shipwreck. It seemed romantic to die in a shipwreck—even though, on reflection, it must be horrible to drown. But I already had enough to think about with Miss Kitty.

Salome had asked for more jasmine tea, and when the nurse did not answer (it must have been the time for the nurses to change shifts), I put the water on to boil on the small desk near the window and poured the tea into the cups. They were very ordinary cups, like those that get stolen from the university canteen, thick stoneware, without any decoration, but I sensed that for Salome they signified something important.

"Tell me more about Miss Kitty!" she said. "And then continue the story of Mr. Cho's pigeons, please?"

She drank her tea in small sips. Her left hand trembled, and her right hand remained resting on her lap, as if it were no longer used for anything. Salome noticed my gaze and said simply, "That's the hardest thing for me to accept, you know." She made a little grimace, as if she was trying to say something funny but failing. "It's leaving bit by bit. Every day, something else goes away, disappears."

I said nothing. I didn't think she needed words to comfort her, or pity. Just the tales, to help her travel.

So every morning Mrs. Lim watched for Miss Kitty's arrival. Sometimes she didn't come, and then the day seemed so long, with the chattering of the hairdressers, and the laments of the clients: "Ah, if you only knew, my son is really bad, sometimes I think he's going to beat me." Or "My husband is going to retire soon, and he wants to travel everywhere, to Manila, Dubai, Mumbai. Everyone says I'm lucky, but none of that appeals to me at all. Quite frankly, I'd rather stay at home and water my flowers." Mrs. Lim did not give a fig for their travels, their sons, or their husbands. She had enough troubles in her own life. So she thought of Miss Kitty, and the answer she would bring in the little bag. When the answer finally arrived, she could wait no longer. She sent away the customers asking for their perms, red dyes, treatments, and scalp massages, closed the shutters, and went to Miss Kitty.

"What have you brought me? Come on, come on."

Miss Kitty held out her neck, and Mrs. Lim gently unfastened the bag. Inside there was a small piece of white paper, on which was written:

She is also my friend.

Mrs. Lim hastily scribbled her reply:

Come and visit me, I'm in the hair salon at the entrance to the apartment complex.

As soon as the little bag was closed, Miss Kitty

moved off. In three bounds she reached the street and hurried away between the bushes in the garden. Without even claiming her due: the plate of fish and the cup of water.

The next day she came back, and there was another message, in different handwriting:

I too am her friend, but I do not live in this building. I just work here, ironing for a couple of elderly people.

Mrs. Lim: *Does anyone know where she lives?*

The answer: *I don't. I think she comes from the ground floor; she takes the elevator up to my floor.*

Then another inquiry, two days later: *Does anyone know what she wants? Does anyone know why she roams?*

And the sarcastic answer (Mrs. Lim thought at once of that grumpy, dirty old man who lived on the ground floor, one of the janitors of the building, no doubt): *She's trying to figure out who she is, obviously. So leave her alone!*

This observation, although it came from an old, half-crazy drunkard, remained in Mrs. Lim's mind, to the point that it became an obsession. *She's trying to figure out who she is.* When she went home after work, instead of sitting in front of the TV and watching her favorite soap operas, she sat in the kitchen thinking. Her husband grew worried.

"What's going on? Are you in trouble?"

Mr. Kang, Mrs. Lim's husband, did not have much imagination. For him everything was either a matter of money problems or health problems. And as Mrs. Lim did not say it was about money, he imagined a more serious cause:

"Honey, why don't you come and sit down? The *Wild Rose* serial is just starting"

Mrs. Lim shrugged. "Leave me alone, I'm thinking."

"Thinking?" Mr. Kang was not sure he had heard right. "Are you sick? Do you need to go see a doctor?"

Three or four years before, Mrs. Lim had discovered a tumor under her right breast, and though the biopsy had eventually revealed that it was just a ball of fat, for a couple of weeks the couple had lived in anguish. Mr. Kang, who was a few years older than his wife, tried to joke to alleviate the anxiety, but it didn't seem to help.

"With all the widows in Seoul," he said, "we'd be doing things wrong if you died first."

Mrs. Lim chuckled. "No, no, darling, don't worry, I'm fine. But it's Miss Kitty . . ." She had talked to him about her once or twice, but Mr. Kang had not been very interested.

"Well, what about this Miss Kitty?"

Mrs. Lim hesitated. Her husband was not the best person to talk to about all this.

"I have a feeling she must have come to the salon for a reason."

"What do you mean?"

"I mean," Ms. Lim began. But the words did not come easily. "It's a kind of impression I have, when she looks at me. I don't know why, but it makes me feel odd, as if she were trying to tell me something."

Mr. Kang was skeptical.

"What a weird idea. What could she possibly be trying to tell you?" He added, proof that he had understood nothing, "If she's troubling you, all you have to do is turn her out of the shop."

He went back to sit down, and since his wife was not watching the soap opera, he changed to another program, the day's political news, repeated in a loop with commentary by a disillusioned-looking journalist.

That night, Mrs. Lim woke up with the impression that she understood some of the mystery, but that impression melted away again when she thought about it seriously.

Miss Kitty had not come by chance. Someone had sent her. She was a messenger, but these messages did not mean much, except that she was going from one person to another in the neighborhood, and that she was beginning to weave a web of relationships between strangers.

Then came the story of Mrs. Yang Yumi, a tenant on the sixth floor of block B.

Mrs. Lim knew her because she had come to the salon once, not to have her hair curled, but to ask for work. Her husband had disappeared without leaving any address, and she had to find some way of surviving, because her only son could not work, having been disabled in an accident. Mrs. Lim felt sorry for Mrs. Yang, but she could neither hire her herself nor find work for her. She had given her some money, which Mrs. Yang had taken, thanking her humbly. Since then, she had heard nothing from her, but she suspected that her situation had not improved. Then one afternoon, around four, Miss Kitty arrived in the salon carrying a message from Mrs. Yang. The message was scribbled on a page torn out of a notepad, in red letters:

I will see you again in a future life, I hope.
Yang Yumi, 6th floor, block B

Mrs. Lim had scarcely read the message before she closed up the salon at full speed, not even taking the time to turn off the lights or stop the hairdryers. She ran to block B with her employees and rushed into the entrance hall. The elevator was at the top of the building, and they had to wait several minutes. As she entered the elevator, Mrs. Lim noticed that Miss Kitty was with them, waiting with them by the door. She seemed to know the way. Had she been sent by Yang Yumi? On the sixth floor, Mrs. Lim hesitated as to which door to knock on. The one on the left, on the right, or in the middle? It was Miss Kitty who indicated the door, and Mrs. Lim began to drum on it. She knocked, then she listened. A noise came from inside the apartment, like a kind of lament, or a sob.

"Open the door, please!" said Mrs. Lim. "We are here to help you. Please open your door!"

A neighbor opened his door. "Why not call the police?" he said, feebly.

Mrs. Lim paid no attention to him, but continued to pound on the door. It was a very ordinary plywood door, with only a decal near the handle, representing a dragon or a phoenix, something of that sort.

"Mrs. Yang, Mrs. Yang, open up, we've come to help you. I'm the hairdresser at the beauty salon, I'm with my employees. We've met before.

After a moment, there was a sound of movement inside the apartment, and Mrs. Lim heard the door being unlocked. Then it opened slowly, as if whoever was inside was pushing something heavy. At that moment, Miss Kitty slipped inside the apartment, and Mrs. Lim heard Mrs. Yang's voice exclaiming, "Ah it's you, you've come back. Thank you, thank you!"

She understood that these words were addressed to none other than Miss Kitty, and she felt a slight sense of vexation, at once forgotten.

Mrs. Lim left the two employees at the entrance of Mrs. Yang's apartment. She did not want too many witnesses. Everything was very dark inside. The blinds were lowered. The floor was littered with newspapers, scraps of paper, and garbage bags stacked in the small corridor, and the living room looked like the scene of a burglary. Almost nothing was in its place, the chairs overturned, vases upside down, bottles of soju and dirty dishes on the floor, and near the window a rolled-up blanket marked where Mrs. Yang slept. Mrs. Lim tried to turn on the light, but it seemed that the power had been cut off, probably after the company had not been paid. When she got used to the darkness, she saw Mrs. Yang sitting on the floor, her back resting against the wall, her hands resting on her thighs, her head bent forward as if she were reading something on the floor. If Mrs. Yang hadn't opened the door herself, Mrs. Lim would have thought she had died on the spot. Just then, Mrs. Lim felt a slight shudder of horror run down her spine, as though she had entered a den full of the supernatural. She sat down beside Mrs. Yang to talk.

"Mrs. Yang, are you all right?"

But it was obvious that she was not all right, far from it. There was a strong smell of alcohol in the apartment. The darkness was full of something agonizing, mortal. Finally, Mrs. Lim's employees came in, and as they came in Mrs. Lim saw Miss Kitty leave the apartment, a furtive yellow streak hastening along the wall on one side.

"Open the blinds!" ordered Mrs. Lim.

Light came pouring into the little room, illuminating the mess, forcing Mrs. Yang to lower her head and hide her face behind her hair, as if the sun hurt her eyes. Her hands were very pale, clenched in her gray hair.

The rest of the evening was spent with Mrs. Yang. The women looked after her, brought her things to drink. One of the employees, the oldest, began to tidy up the small apartment, to make piles of all that had to be thrown away, all that had to be forgotten. Mrs. Yang allowed it, lying on the floor with her mouth open as if catching her breath after a deep-water dive. She had said nothing, nothing intelligible, but it was evident that she had wanted to die, by opening the gas of her stove, perhaps, or by swallowing bleach—there was a can half full near the door, the plug unscrewed. Or perhaps by jumping out of the window, seeing that the door to the small balcony was ajar. All evening, and even for part of the night, the women stayed together. Mr. Kang phoned, and even came to see them, and for once he seemed quite emotional. He brought a small flowerpot for Mrs. Yang, with some barely open daffodils, and Mrs. Yang gazed at them as if they were the most wonderful thing in the world.

Then, over the following days, ordinary life resumed, but Mrs. Lim did not stop coming to see Mrs. Yang. Finally, she found a little job for her, in a sewing workshop not far from the Good Luck! complex. It was as if all the women of the neighborhood had taken an oath to keep each other informed of their doings. To remain united, even if there was no threat weighing over them. To talk to each other, send messages on their mobile phones, or even make small unexpected visits. The only sadness Mrs. Lim felt, and this was shared by all the people in the neighborhood, was that from that memorable evening when Mrs. Yang had decided to die, Miss Kitty had disappeared. She never returned to the salon with her messages. Mr. Kang's explanation was that she had found another place, less agitated, with fewer dramas. Cats like their tranquility, it's well known. But Mrs. Lim thought of another reason, a little crazy it is true, but which explained a lot: Miss Kitty, the Traveler, was no ordinary cat. She was a goddess, a ghost, or something of that kind.

If Mrs. Lim had been a Christian, she would have said that Miss Kitty was an angel, or if Miss Kitty had been black-haired instead of blonde, a demon. But Mrs. Lim identified more with Buddhism, and this meant that for her Miss Kitty was truly a traveler, going through several lives, several worlds, to carry out her work of reparation, perhaps in expiation of a fault committed in her youth, when she had let her younger sister die of despair. Mrs. Lim remembered hearing a story—not in the Good Luck! complex, and not in block B, but mentioned on television, or in the newspapers—about a young woman, a singer, who had been found hanging in her apartment, in the midst of disorder and empty bottles of soju. But maybe it was only a story, one of those legends that hatch in the neighborhoods of this city where every minute a host of things happen, bizarre, beautiful, or terrible, as you wished to see it.

For some time, I stopped coming to see Salome. I hadn't forgotten her, but my studies, and the seminars I had to organize three evenings a week, were eating into my time. I hadn't touched the envelope containing the 50,000 won bills, perhaps because I felt obliged to continue what I had begun, or perhaps because of the woman on the bills, the great lady, looking a little sad, who made me think of Salome. It was as if the bills were saying, "Don't forget me. Come and see me!" Or even, in Salome's grave voice, "Don't be so cruel!" The salary for the seminars was sufficient to pay my rent, and for the rest, I managed. I ate mainly *ramyeon* and kimchi. I remember my grandmother once claimed that you could survive by eating only kimchi morning, noon, and night! This, she said, was the diet after the war years, when, to punish Jeolla-do, the government of Syngman Rhee had obliged its inhabitants, suspected of being Communist insurgents, to follow a famine diet.

Besides, there was something new in my life. During an excursion with friends, I had bumped into Mr. Pak, the young man from the bookstore in Jongno, and we began going out together sometimes. I learned his name, which was not Mr. Pak but Mr. Ko. He came from Jeju Island. However, I continued to call him by the name I had invented, in order not to have to correct my memory. He had given himself a Christian name, Frederick, in memory of Frederic Chopin, because he was very fond of piano music.

Naturally, we talked about Salome. He did not know her well, he said. He met her when he brought her books she had ordered, novels in English and French, and scientific books on medicine and psychology. Speaking with her, he had thought maybe I could become her companion, not someone to talk to her and change her ideas, but someone who could share with her an imaginary world. When you're sick, he said, the world becomes entirely imaginary. I didn't think he was wrong. Without my being able to resist, his face came to haunt my days and nights. I liked everything about him, especially his almond-shaped eyes, of a very bright black, lined with ordinary eyelashes. And his eyebrows—I remembered that my mother always used to say that what made pretty boys prettiest was well-arched eyebrows, as if drawn with charcoal. I liked the color of his skin, brown, almost reddish, and his hair, which was cut short. I liked his long, strong hands, and the square tips of his fingers. He confessed one day that he was not patient enough to cut his fingernails into rounds, so he cut them straight across with scissors, in three quick snips, *click, click, clack*!

We got into the habit of seeing one another several times a week, every weekend, and whenever he got off work in the early afternoon. We walked in a different place each time, beside the river, or the gardens in the city center, or, when the weather was nice, the zoo south of the city. I had always liked visiting the zoo, not because of the animals you could see in the cages—in fact, I remember very well that when I was a child, I made a solemn oath that one day I would open the cages in all the zoos, to restore liberty to those prisoners who had done nothing wrong. Rather, I liked it for the gardens, winding lanes lined with palm trees and camellias, and also for the people who went there, the children running and screaming, old folk trying to catch them to give them something to eat, and also, of course, the lovebird couples sitting in the shade in the more isolated corners.

Now I was there, too, with a boy. We walked along the avenues, not really talking, just engaged in the ordinary chit-chat of sweethearts trying to get to know each other better.

"Frederick," I said (I had recently begun to use

his English name), "is it true that lovers like to meet beside the water?"

"Where did you read that?"

"I don't know," I said. "I've never been in love." After reflection, I added, "I think there is some truth in the saying, because water is a romantic element. In all love stories there is water, either the sea or a river, or even just a lake, or a pool."

"It could also be a swimming pool," Frederick said, laughing.

I didn't dare tell him then, but from the very start I had wanted him to take me to the seaside. Seoul, this huge city, was so dry, nothing but buildings and roads, cars and buses.

We went instead to the zoo, all the way to the green monkey pen, because even if they are prisoners, green monkeys seem to enjoy themselves, arguing, shouting, making love, and stealing food from one another, just like humans. They might just as well be living in a city.

As we walked towards the center of the garden, the cries of monkeys and birds echoed over the trees, and it made me feel I was walking in a dream, far away from the troubles of reality, far from the nastiness of my aunt and her horrible daughter.

We took pictures using Frederick's phone. These were silly pictures like everybody takes, selfies where we stood cheek to cheek, and I was doing the V sign or making a little heart with my hands, who knows why. Then he decorated them with hearts and clouds in which he had written, of course, *sarang*—love. On one of the pictures he wrote the prettiest thing anyone had ever written to me: *Bitna, my Star!* I remembered what my mother had told me once, that it was my maternal grandfather who had chosen my name, which means "Shine," because he wanted me to shine in my life, both within and without.

We stayed in the zoo until closing time, simply walking through the crowds, listening to the shouts of the children, the screams of the monkeys, and the shrieks of the parrots. I felt free, for the first time in a long time. I did idiotic things that I would not have thought myself capable of, like swinging on the gates, or running around the pools, or singing loudly, songs by Gummy, and Ed Sheeran, and others. As someone who loved beautiful piano music, symphonies, and the *lieder* of Schubert, Frederick looked embarrassed, and that was precisely what amused me. He was always a bit stiff. Even when dressed in jeans and a jacket, he looked like he was wearing a suit. But that was also something I loved. I would not have liked him to become like those *wangja*, "little kings" who perfumed themselves and spent their time putting on hairspray. Frederick reassured me. He looked sure of himself, sure about what he wanted in life. In this he was completely different from me. I never knew what tomorrow would bring.

It was the money, I think, that started to preoccupy me. In the beginning, Frederick invited me everywhere. He was the one who always paid, in the restaurants, in the cafés, or in the taxis. Once he asked me a question, and I felt embarrassed.

"Bitna, how is it working out for you, your studies?"

"I like my French classes," I said.

He smiled. "No, I mean, in terms of money?"

"I'm all right, I don't really have any money problems." I kept lying. "My family is not very rich, but they support me, and I add to that with odd jobs."

I didn't want him to know that I only ate kimchi, and I especially didn't want him to see the neighborhood I was living in.

I was evasive.

"I have a small room in a dormitory near Hongik University. It's not luxurious, but it's comfortable."

"No roommate?"

"Oh no, I would not like that at all. Students are all so dirty, and they snore!"

It was at this time that I began to invent the details of my life for him, to throw him off the scent. His own life was so well ordered. He lived with his parents in a nice neighborhood. He was working toward a master's degree in economics, and at the same time, he was working his sales job in Jongno. He was going to buy a car soon. It was going to be a gift from his parents when he graduated from university.

So I had to become what he imagined me to be, a young girl of the bourgeoisie, father a civil servant, mother a teacher at a private middle school, with nothing to do with Jeolla-do or fish. Though I did eventually tell him about my grandmother, who had come from the north, lost her husband during the war, and been a refugee in Busan.

These weren't lies. They were to me the continuation of the stories that I told Salome, in order to see her eyelids become weighed down with sleep, or to make her heart beat.

Frederick and I had a rather strange relationship, for we never talked about our real lives. In fact, I didn't know anything about him. When we separated, we would take a taxi. He dropped me off first in front of the university, where I was supposed to live, then he continued on. He never gave the driver his address in my presence. Once, I asked him about this. I think it was a bit to tease him, and a little bit out of curiosity—girls are always a little curious, and even excessively nosy.

"Take me to where you live. I'd like to see your neighborhood."

He looked embarrassed.

"It's not a good idea, I live a long way away, and people might see me with you."

His reply felt like a little stab to my heart. He must have realized it, because he tried to explain.

"It's my parents. They know a lot of people in the neighborhood, and you know how tongues wag when there's something to talk about."

I didn't much like this explanation. I would have preferred him to have invited me to meet his precious parents—even though I would have refused to go. But I cut him short.

"It's all right, you don't need to explain. I understand perfectly."

On the other hand, I never even tried to tell him about my family problems. I only mentioned Jeolla-do once, and I neglected to mention my aunt and her daughter

Baekhwa. The very idea that he might meet them one day seemed absurd. In my mind, the apartment where I had lived with them was a nest of scorpions.

We continued to go out together, Frederick and I, and take great walks through the city. He liked the monuments. We visited the old temples up in the hills, and also the museums. Although I was never really interested in architecture, I patiently listened to his explanations about the corbels and the intertwining of old tiles. We ended the walks with visits to the cafés in Hongdae or Sinchon, the ones with a terrace where Frederick could light up a cigarette. I resumed my habit of smoking with him. We bought menthol cigarettes, the ones you pinched between thumb and index finger to release the mint extract into the tobacco.

We drank very dark coffee. For me, coffee and tobacco were the symbols of this boy, not only because of the color of his eyes and his skin, but also because there was something obscure and bitter about him that fascinated me. We lingered on the terraces, ignoring the ordinary comings and goings of the local students, smoking and sipping our coffee, almost without speaking. I would have loved more intimacy, but he refused. No doubt for fear of being seen by others. In the same way, although we had become closer—we had begun to flirt seriously in the gardens, or on the banks beside the river—Frederick refused to hold hands. We should never express our feelings. This was his idea of life as a couple.

"Other people don't need to know," he said.

In the same way, he was the one who decided when we would meet.

"Not tomorrow, or the day after. I'll be busy," he would say.

"What if I only have time on those days?"

He looked at me without any emotion.

"Then it'll all be over."

It was up to me to give in, to change my schedule. I missed several seminars as a result, and was in danger of losing the pay that went with them.

Frederick never explained the reasons for his refusals. He worked, though obviously, it was not the same kind of work. I didn't have any obligations to a team. I didn't have to do accounting, or be involved in updating the inventory of the bookstore.

He explained to me one day, "I'm only doing this job for the experience. My goal is finance. I want to enter a big group. Samsung, LG, or Hyundai. I'm not going to spend my whole life with books."

That hurt me a little, since I wanted nothing more than to spend my life with books.

I had neglected Salome for many weeks. She sent me messages on my phone, at first light ones, saying, *I need Mr. Cho Hansu and his pigeons, or the story of Kitty, quickly!* Then more and more desperate. *Don't forget your Kim Seri, she will die!* Or *Tell me a story, a story to send me to sleep forever!*

The outings with Frederick were becoming expensive. I needed money, and the studio owner was demanding my three months of back rent. In spite of all my fine principles, I had used up the beautiful bills in the envelopes, the ones with the sad-looking lady, in restaurants and outings. I felt a kind of impatience now. I no longer worried about the fate of the lady on the bill, or anything else. Life in this great city was similar to a large orphanage I had once visited with a student from an English course, where dozens of babies were waiting, as if in a market, to be bought by a rich family without descendants, who would be very careful not to adopt a child with Down's syndrome or the child of drug addicts.

I answered Salome's calls. I chose a day when Frederick Pak was away, and I went to the southern part of the city.

The third story I told Salome

July 2016

In the maternity ward, the little darlings are lined up, each in its cradle. For the moment, all are sleeping, and nothing is moving. Behind the window, a little clouded by their breaths, the nurse Hana is nearly asleep on her chair. It is still dark outside, as can be seen by the blue of the barred windows, but the big room is brightly lit by a dozen neon tubes, some of which are flashing, at the end of their lives, giving off a cold, white light.

This is where Naomi arrived, one morning in July 2009. It was Hana who first found Naomi, after arriving at the Maternity Hospital of the Good Shepherd. Hana went on duty at six in the morning. She had arrived at Hongik University Station and was going up the lane toward the top of the hill. At six o'clock, the streets were still deserted, littered in places with boxes and empty bottles left by revelers the night before. Hana was used to this state of things. She no longer groaned as she had at first ("Wretched students, living like dogs, as they like, without thought for others!").

When she arrived in front of the door of the clinic, the first thing she saw was a pile of rags on the ground. She was about to push it toward the gutter with her foot when the pile of rags started to move, and she heard small cries, rather like those from a litter of kittens. She leaned carefully over the rags and parted them with her fingertips, in case there was an animal inside ready to scratch and bite her. Then she saw it—a tiny baby, pink-skinned, eyes closed, with a tuft of very black hair. Naomi.

Of course, she was not called Naomi then. It was Hana who gave her the name. She had never married, never had a child, but she had always thought that if she had had a child, it would have been a girl, and she would have called her Naomi.

A month has passed since Naomi had arrived. Now her eyes are open, and she lives in her cradle, in the middle of the nursery room, with twenty-six other babies. She's the most beautiful, the other nurses often say, and Hana agrees with them. The babies are of different ages. Some have been there for six months, and some arrived after Naomi. There are boys and girls. Some are handicapped, and that is already clear despite their young age. All of them have been abandoned by their mothers, for a variety of reasons, mostly because the mother was very young, still almost a child, and likely unable to care for a baby or, above all, face the shame of having had a child outside the bounds of marriage. Every day, would-be parents visit the maternity ward to adopt a baby. They have no right to choose, not even to come close. They are content to stay behind the large window overlooking the nursery. From there they watch the cradles and listen to the babies' cries. Maybe they hope to feel a call, just by looking at the little beds and listening to the crying babies, and guessing how the child would turn out later. Hana has placed Naomi in the very center of the room, as far as possible from the window, hoping that potential adoptive parents will not see her, not notice her voice, and not be seduced by her pink skin and her pretty black hair.

What can Naomi see? She still cannot move her head. It is too heavy, glued to the cold sheet over the mattress. But her eyes are wide open, watching the clouds of light that pass above her, sometimes very white, hiding everything in their moving curls, sometimes barely visible, like tulle, a light gauze scattered through the room and sparkling in the millions of droplets suspended in the air. But Naomi is the only one who sees them. And she also feels the presence of the other babies. There are many, but the number doesn't mean anything to her. It's all of the cries, the tears, and then also the breaths, the smell of sweat and urine, the slightly acrid smell of suckling babes, smells that trace a checkerboard pattern on the ceiling, on the walls, even on the invisible floor. And then there's something else, it looks like a wave, a cry, a color, but it's none of those. It comes and goes, crosses Naomi's space, slides over her body, her closed face, her belly, inside her hands and feet. A wave, maybe. Naomi feels the presence of all the bodies around her, even when they stop crying and weeping, even when they have fallen asleep for sheer weariness, even when they are forgotten. Naomi feels a vibration inside her body telling her that she is a girl, the daughter of a woman, launched into the world from that moment on, and she knows this will never leave her for a moment, for the rest of her life, for all the years that have to be lived, yes, until the end, until the last moment.

Naomi, little Naomi, listen to me, smile at me. I'm here for you, my dear.

Hana is leaning over the bed. She gazes into the baby's very large and very black eyes, where the whites are still blue from the night before her birth.

Where have you come from, little Naomi? Do you remember? Will you be able to say one day? Who brought you into the world, then abandoned you on the steps of the Good Shepherd, wrapped in a pile of old rags, clean but not enough to make a dress or even a bed. Who laid you there in the early morning of approaching spring with the pollen of cherry blossoms on your lips and the acrid odor of the grass growing in the park? Did you see the cranes from Siberia crossing the sea to Japan? They advance slowly, the oldest at their head, in perfect order, and then you hear their hollow cries echoing through the city, down to the very bottom of the lanes of Sinchon and Hongdae, into your hiding place at the foot of the gray building. Do you remember, little Naomi? This is the beginning of your life, you cannot forget that. You were not born in a hospital like the other babies, you were born somewhere in the city, in a garden perhaps, or on the flat roof of a house, amidst boxes and drying sheets. You cried out at the same time as your mother who was bringing you into the world, and then you came here to the threshold of the clinic so that I could find you, and make you mine.

But Naomi is not listening. She is still in the other world, that which is before birth, which humans carry about with them, attached to their cord, to their limbs, to their sex, a world so vast and so unknown that the mind cannot conceive of it, because the mind is just that little piece of flesh, and time and space are attached to it for just a few moments, a few days, a few weeks, as if through a minute orifice we could see the beginning of infinity.

Listen to my voice, it's the first voice you heard, for those who brought you and left you on the steps of the clinic did so in silence. They were so afraid that one day you might remember, might recognize their voices and shout at them, "Wretches, what have you done? Why did you forsake me?" My voice when I found you. Immediately I took you in my arms. I, Hana, already old, who could never have children, whose womb is dry and sterile and breasts empty as old wrinkled wineskins. My voice. I sang when I took you up to rock you in my arms. I sang a song without words, the one that my mother sang to me when I was born, I

remember, the song I asked of her when we left the
south to come to this great city, and I was afraid of
losing my way.

No words, simply, lu lulu lululu, lu, lu lulu lu, lu,
lululu, lu . . . *Very softly rounding her mouth, so that*
the words are like the cooing of pigeons on a roof.
My dove, so that you may remember, so that you
know that there was someone there already, in the
cold streets, in the spring wind, in the smell of the

grass in the park, in the white clouds of cherry blos-
soms, in the rustle of the raindrops that morning.

After that, the main ward of the clinic receives little Naomi.

A new bed is rolled out onto the tiles, a bed with four walls of cloth, a hard mattress over which the sheet is stretched like a drum skin. Naomi is laid on the bed. She cries, and all the babies cry with her. She suddenly hears human voices. It's scary, and at the same time it's the beginning of an adventure—all of these babies, abandoned by desperate unmarried mothers, by absent or terri-fied fathers, by families blinded by egoism and baseness, by institutions, by laws, and by habits. Babies, like small animals, greedy and ferocious, already attached to life with all their limbs, with all their nerves.

Salome did not like this story. She had wanted a sequel to the other stories, or intrigue, something that would satisfy her appetite. Or maybe it was because the story reminded her of her own history. Her parents had abandoned her. They had left her a considerable fortune, and then taken poison and gone to join their ancestors.

"Why do we know nothing about these babies? Why do their birth mothers abandon them? What will become of them?"

"You'd like to know, wouldn't you?" All of a sudden, I realized that I had a kind of power over her, a bit like how Frederick had power over me. It was a feeling both agreeable and venomous, the impression of yielding to a temptation, to a vice. To make sure, I added, "If you do not like my stories, we can stop now."

Salome lowered her head. I was her only link with the outside world, a gratuitous, immaterial link, nothing to do with the usual ballet of nurses and caregivers who changed her diapers, washed her, fed her, and helped her lie down.

She whispered, "No, please, stay, tell me whatever you like."

So I continued the story of Naomi.

In her cold little bed, she was mostly silent. When the other babies began crying, one, then another, then three, then ten, then the whole room, crying loudly, their little faces closed like fists, their throats open in shrill screams, their skin turning dark red, the nurses came rushing in. They ran along the spaces between the cots, unable to do anything, passing from one to the other, feeling the diapers, checking the mattresses to see if there was not a forgotten pin, then blocking their ears so as not to go mad.

What they did not know was that it was I who had launched the call to cry. When all was silent—not at night, because in the clinic, night does not exist, only the subdued light from the nightlights along the plinths—I felt an anguish rising in me, the anguish of the babies that people abandon in the same way they drown small kittens.

Then I uttered a cry, a single cry, but shrill, malicious, a cry for help, or a cry of rage, and the entire nursery awoke and followed suit, crying until the nurses, even the assistants and the midwives, came running.

Old Hana knew. She quickly realized, by instinct, or because she had been the first to hear me cry when she picked me up on the steps of the clinic that morning. But she did not betray me. She understood me. I was her baby, and nobody else's. She could not accept that strangers might arrive, their faces delicately powdered, and take me to their beautiful houses in Gangnam, or to their luxurious apartments at the edge of the Hangang River. It was she who invented the rumor that I was an abnormal child, that I was deaf, that I had Down Syndrome, that I suffered from nervous attacks. When the candidates for adoption came up to the other side of the window and they spotted my cradle, having seen from afar that I had a lot of hair and very pink skin, Hana intervened.

"You know that that baby is not like the others, don't you? I suppose you were told at the adoption office?"

If they insisted, "But we will give her a lot of love, because she needs more than the others," she replied, "That child will never talk, will never smile, in fact we are not quite sure if she can see. It seems she has problems in that area."

Hana continued to discourage the applicants, until the day when the management decided they could no longer keep Naomi, that she was causing too much trouble in the clinic, and that because of her, many other babies had not been adopted. What was to be done with her? There was some question of entrusting her to a state institution for handicapped children. Hana was prepared. She announced that she would soon be leaving the clinic to return to the south, to look after her mother. A few days before the end of her service, she managed to take the night watch, from one o'clock in the morning to six o'clock. She prepared everything she would need for the following days. And that night, Naomi decided to aim high. She remained calm for long hours, until all the nurses on duty had fallen asleep in their chairs in front of the television. Then, at exactly five thirty, Naomi uttered the most strident, atrocious cry she had ever uttered. Chaos erupted, with everyone running in all directions, eyes puffy with sleep, trying to put an end to the din of babies all screaming in chorus. Hana took advantage of the confusion to wrap Naomi in a blanket, then she slipped out. She pushed open the front door of the hospital, and outside she saw a black taxi waiting for her, lights on. She felt a great joy. She opened the door of the car, and sat down in the back seat, hugging little Naomi.

"Where are we going?" asked the driver.

"Straight ahead!" was Hana's only response.

When the car started, Hana leaned back in her seat and pulled aside the blanket. The light of the dawning day was not enough for her to be certain, but it seemed to her that Naomi was smiling.

The continuation of the history of Mr. Cho and his pigeons
Late July 2016

Every morning at dawn Mr. Cho took his scooter, loaded up with two or three cages of pigeons, and carefully chose a site near the river where he could train the pigeons to cross the river in a single stretch, without stopping at the islets or under the piers of the bridges. In the morning at daybreak the great river resembled a serpent of clouds. The mist came up from the sea along the estuary. Next, near Incheon, the pigeons learned to fly over the stretches of red grass that the sea water slowly invaded with the rising tide.

To the claw of Black Dragon, Mr. Cho attached a rolled-up message, consisting of isolated words, of which he alone knew the meaning, such as:

sea
  island
     wind
    wing
return

And from the right claw of Diamond, he hung soft messages full of love,

infinite
   long time
caress

and also the name of his wife, Han Seonhee. Mr. Cho often thought of her. She had died down on the island when he was still in the police force. Since he hadn't earned much, she had worked as a *ttaemiri*, a scrubber in a public bathhouse, massaging and scouring the skin of the village women.

It was for her that Mr. Cho began his adventure with the pigeons. He remembered her saying one day, "You'd have to be a bird to go back there." Obviously. The watchtowers and the barbed wire only stopped terrestrial animals and human beings. Birds and insects, perhaps even snakes and frogs, could not be stopped by the demarcation line. It was with the money his wife earned that they were able to raise all these pigeons. She had come to share his dream of sending a message one day to his family on the other side. But she had died before it could be realized.

After the tests over the great river, Mr. Cho decided that mountain trials were also necessary. Over there, on the other side, were high, snow-capped mountains, sharp peaks and deep crevasses, which would be impassable obstacles to any that did not know how to fly well. For the initial training, Mr. Cho took his pigeons to the top of Bukhansan Mountain. It would be too taxing to try to get there on his scooter—it was old, and he had used it mostly in the days when he transported vegetables and fruit from the markets to the city centers—so Mr. Cho thought it more prudent to use the services of a taxi. He negotiated the price, for an early morning transfer and the return trip at the end of the day. The driver, named Mr. Yi, was, like Mr. Cho, a former policeman, so the deal was made with full confidence, for a very reasonable price. The only thing Mr. Yi demanded was that the birds travel in the trunk, which he would keep partially open, to avoid any bad smells and feathers inside his vehicle. Mr. Cho accepted without hesitation.

"The pigeons are not sensitive. A little fresh air will do them good," he said.

This time, Mr. Cho had prepared more explicit messages, in case one of the birds got lost in the mountains and was taken in by a local inhabitant. They said *Hello! My name is Black Dragon, I am carrying a message to be returned exclusively to my master, Mr. Cho,* followed by his address. He would have added his daughter's phone number, but he was afraid that his daughter might not want her personal number to fall into the hands of strangers, and she still laughed at him because of his fancy.

So one morning early in April, Mr. Yi's taxi dropped off Mr. Cho near the top of the mountain. The wind was cold, but above the mist the sky shone a spotless blue.

"Come along, my dears," said Mr. Cho to his pair of pigeons. "You are going to experience flying in the purest air this country has to offer, far from the city."

He opened the cage first, to accustom the birds to their mission. At the same time, he made cooing sounds at the back of his throat to reassure them. He first took out Diamond, holding her tightly in his hands, gently blowing on her beak, and she struggled a little, because she had smelled the delicious fragrance of the air, the pine woods in the sun, the small juicy plants between the stones, and maybe even the snow, which had a calm odor that only birds could detect. The next moment, Mr. Cho walked to the low wall from where he could look out over the landscape stretching below and threw Diamond into the air. He watched her fly high, pass the rising sun, and then turn above the trees. The sound of her wings filled the still air. Immediately afterwards, Mr. Cho freed Black Dragon, and he rose vertically, in a hurried flapping of wings, eager to rejoin his companion.

The two birds found one another in the sky and began to circle each other, so close and so rapid that Mr. Cho feared for a moment that they would smash into the surrounding rocks. Then he closed his eyes in order to better feel what they were feeling, a kind of hurricane of light and wind, making the mountain turn beneath them, plaiting together the threads of white and gray clouds.

Salome closed her eyes too. She stretched out her hand and clasped mine, as if I could pass through my skin the taste of the air at the top of the mountain, the sound of the wind in the pines, the rustling of the wings of the pigeons. She shuddered, because her illness had multiplied her nerve endings, and the slightest breath passing over her made all her cells vibrate. It was Yuri, my doctor friend, who first told me about complex regional pain syndrome, Salome's condition.

"At a certain point in the disease, the slightest sensation becomes an intolerable source of pain; we have to resort to sedatives."

She had said this with complete medical detachment, but here, in the room with the curtains drawn against the light, suffocating with silence, I felt like I could perceive what Salome felt, a sort of electric wave over her skin, in her body, the roots of her hair.

I whispered, "I'm sorry, Salome, I did not mean to hurt you. I can go if you want."

She didn't answer, but her hand curled, and her fingers with their hooked nails clung to me and dug into my flesh, and her thin lips turned blue.

Right. Now it was time for my story. I didn't invent it. It really happened to me.

I decided to relate it to Salome, because, at a certain point, I grew tired of telling her stories about a too-perfect world.

Of course, Salome was seriously ill. She couldn't move from her chair, she wore diapers, and her skin was like rough paper stained red and blue. Her smell too, was something I had difficulty accepting. Before that, I didn't know that sick people had a smell. It was a bit acidic, like that of old people. I knew the smell of old people because for a long time, when I was a child, I gave my grandmother massages. But with old people, the smell was softer, a little like faded flowers. Salome's smell was strong, acrid. She smelled like an animal, mingled with sweat. Her nurse poured liters of cologne over her neck in vain. The smell floated up and rose to the surface. Sometimes I wanted to say, "Salome, you smell bad!" I didn't tell her, not out of respect, or because she paid me (after all, I was not her servant, I was her storyteller). No, it was rather out of pride, because I believed that I had no right to complain, and that I could not change anything anyway. Either I kept coming, or I didn't. But what was the point of chatter?

However, the smell was deep inside me. When I went home to my small basement apartment, I opened the fanlight that was level with the street, even if there were garbage bags that attracted rats and cockroaches. I lay down on the mattress on the floor, and the smell returned, it filled the room, it filled my nostrils. Sometimes I even wondered if I was producing the smell myself. I put my head under the blanket and fell asleep, clenching my fists.

That was how the "wannabe" murderer came along.

Story of an apprentice murderer
Early August 2016

At the time, I was still living near Ewha Womans University, where small streets climbed the hill. The area was occupied by two-story apartment buildings that looked rather sordid, and when friends at university asked me where I lived, I said, "The name of the neighborhood is El Sordido." It could have been the name of my building, too, which had no name, just a number, building 203, room 1002. Built of bricks and concrete blocks, with metal windows and doors, and an almost vertical staircase with no lighting. The ground floor was occupied by a *seolleongtang* soup restaurant, the upper floor by a massage parlor. I was given free rein of the semi-basement, which had a single window and a fanlight at the level of the street, often obstructed by trash bags. At the start, I had to wage a desperate battle (I was the most desperate part of it) against a big rat that had grown used to frequenting my room. It entered through the air duct and had forced open the grating. I replaced the grating with a piece of wood, but the rat gnawed at it every night. I tried putting a piece of plaster in its place, but that did not resist the rat's teeth. As a final solution, I bought a piece of zinc from a second-hand store, which I nailed to the wall, but the nights that followed were hell, because the big rat (I called it Fat Boy, without being sure that it was not a Fat Girl) was trying to gnaw a hole through the zinc, and the sound of its incisors on the metal made for strident music that kept me awake until morning. The dealer who had sold me the zinc felt sorry for me.

"There's only one remedy against rats," he said.

I assumed he was talking about poison.

"No, your rat knows all about poison. It won't touch it, and it's dangerous for children."

He gave me pieces of a broken glass soju bottle wrapped in newspaper.

"You grind that up and mix it with rice. It'll eat it and die."

It was a cruel remedy, but I thought it was either the rat or me. A few nights passed, and I heard nothing more of the rat, so I imagined that it had gone outside to die in a dark corner.

The rat was only a start. Sometime later, I was the victim of a more dramatic attack. I was sleeping on my mattress when I was awoken by the sense of a strange presence. I took it for a bad dream, but when I turned my head toward the window, I thought my heart was going to stop. On the other side of the glass, a man was crouching, looking in at me. I had imagined that nobody could see me, given the location of the window, close to the level of the street, and for that reason I had not put up any curtains. It was high summer, stiflingly hot, and I had opened the window a chink. I could distinctly hear the man breathing, and even see the two halos of mist that his nostrils left on the pane.

I do not know how long I stayed there, para-lyzed, looking at the man's silhouette, like in a bad dream where you dare not even breathe. Then a scream rose from my throat. I cried out with all my might, loud enough to deafen myself in the little room, and the man fled. What could I do? Complain to the police? But nothing had happened, and I didn't even have a description to give them. Just a silhouette, pressed against my window, the sound of his breathing, the impres-sion of his gaze. I could not talk about it, not even to the dealer at the second-hand shop. Did he also have a cure to get rid of stalkers? The following night I covered the window with newspaper pages taped onto the glass, I even placed the room's only armchair against the door handle, but I could not sleep. From time to time, when I fell asleep, I distinctly heard knocking at the pane, small rapid, impatient knocks. I burrowed under my blanket to stop hearing.

I started noticing that it wasn't only at night. When I went out of my basement room to go to class, or to work in the library, I felt as if I was being followed. The El Sordido area was perfect for that. Those little streets that went tumbling down to the subway station, the dark corners, the drive-ways, the inner courtyards—everything looked dubious to me, and I saw suspicious silhouettes everywhere. I ran without looking back. I turned left, then right, then I stopped, using the reflection in the window of the pharmacy to see what was behind me. A black silhouette was there behind me, a tall, strong man, with drooping shoulders, wearing wrinkled pants and a gray shirt, his head stuffed into a woolen cap in spite of the heat. Now I knew everything about him, without ever having seen him face to face. My panic once past, I decided to counterattack by identifying the maximum of elements needed for a description. For his height, I evaluated the height of an ad pasted on an electricity pole, and still looking in the reflection in the window, I saw that he exceeded the mark by a dozen centimeters, which made him approximately one meter eighty tall. As for his weight, this was more uncertain. I chose to slip between some boxes lying close together on the sidewalk, and I saw that he could not follow the same path, and had to step down onto the roadway. His age was also uncertain, but he was able to run, or walk with great strides, and I was sure that he was in the prime of life—that is to say, formidable.

Why had he chosen me? No doubt he had spotted me long before I realized it, when I first arrived in this cursed neighborhood, in this basement, when I had fled from my aunt's apartment. But why did he persist in following me? To confuse him, I changed my habits. Until then I had slept late, staying awake a long time reading and studying in the room with the light on, and when I woke up, it was usually already close to noon, the day already underway for quite some time. So I started to turn off my light early, to make him believe that

I was sleeping, and I got used to waking up very early. Sometimes I was out by six in the morning, without eating anything, or even taking the time to brush my teeth. I went out wearing the previous day's clothes. I did not change, nor brush my hair. I wanted to look so pitiful that no one would want to speak to me. At first, I thought he had understood, that he had given up. Then, just as I was going down the subway stairs, I turned around and there he was, at the top of the alley, his hands in his pockets, his wool cap always pulled down over his big round head, and I even saw he was smiling. And that smile sent a shiver down my spine, as if from far off he had slid a knife over my skin.

Salome listened to my story without flinching. I think she, too, felt fear. Maybe she, too, had never thought about it before, that someone could follow a girl in the street, without speaking, without approaching her, just for the sheer pleasure of causing fear. I reproached myself for telling her all this, upsetting her expectations. Was it to avenge myself on her, on her so cozy and protected world, where despite her illness, money was never lacking, where nurses succeeded each other regularly, to serve her, to whom I now belong, since I am bound to speak to her? Or was it because I wanted to punish her for being as she is, defenseless, wrapped in her death-smell?

"I'm sorry," I told her. "I shouldn't be telling you all this. I can see that you don't like my story."

"No, no, Bitna, please." She protested, her cheeks suddenly on fire, her eyes shining. "It's a story, isn't it? All of that doesn't really exist?"

For a moment, I was tempted to say to her, "Do you think I'm capable of inventing a murderer?" But I said instead, "No, no, Salome, of course it's a story, like the one about the cat who carries messages, and Mr. Cho with his pigeons."

But I hesitated before answering, and Salome interjected to break the silence instead of waiting for my reply. Maybe, like me, she wanted to believe that it wasn't true, but at the same time, she wanted to know more, because even lies have some truth hidden in them.

The rainy season arrived suddenly, with torrents of rain pouring down over the city, and rivers flowing along the streets. It was my first experience of this kind of rain, because in Jeolla-do, when it rains, the earth immediately absorbs streams and pools, but here, in Sinchon, it was a little bit like the end of the world. The sky was filled with thick rolling clouds that hid the top of the buildings. The crossroads were drowned, with geysers spouting from the manholes. Every day, to go to university, or to give my language classes, I had to confront disaster. An umbrella was useless. I wrapped my backpack in several plastic bags and sheltered myself as best I could under a sailor's oilskin (it was all I had left from my youthful days in the fish market). I took off my shoes and carried them in my hand. The advantage of having grown up in a rural village was that you got used to going barefoot. Meanwhile I saw other students stumbling along on their high heels, which sank in the mud, or sliding around in flip-flops, flapping their arms like birds on pack ice. I always enjoyed walking barefoot in the rain, feeling the water seeping between my toes. It brought back memories of childhood sensations. The rainy season also gave me respite, because the silhouette of my stalker had disappeared. No doubt he did not like being wet, or, being less skilled than I was, he could no longer manage to keep up with me in streets and alleys swept into torrents.

I stopped seeing Mr. Pak around that time. It just happened, just like that, without thinking. He was supposed to phone me and did not. I was supposed to go see him at the bookstore one Saturday afternoon, and I went to the cinema instead, alone, to watch a thriller. It was as if the absence of the stalker had motivated the disappearance of my boyfriend. Or as if the two were simply two faces of the same personage—a domineering and narcissistic, slightly selfish man on the one hand, and a dangerous and greedy stranger on the other.

I hadn't seen Salome for some time either. I didn't call her. Because of the rainy season, I suppose. And then there was my work helping to prepare the French courses at the university. I accepted the job even though the pay was peanuts. It was Younja, the Bitch, who had offered it to me. It wasn't entirely legal, because I didn't have the necessary diplomas, but I made her believe that I had lived a long time in Africa and spoke French like a native. Besides, it was convenient for her, because she and her husband had decided to have a child, and she

106

couldn't work because she was busy undergoing a whole series of tests. Of course, at forty, she was already running out of time, but I had no sympathy for her. First, because she was and would forever be a Bitch, always arrogant and sure of herself, and of the family fortune (her father owned the largest rice cake factory in Seoul, and was starting to export to African countries), and then because she only gave me a small part of the salary she received from the university to take her place. I know I could threaten to denounce her, but what would I gain by that? She would keep her place, thanks to her dad's money, and I would have the reputation of being the Bitch—the ungrateful backbiter. So, I went to campus every day to prepare lectures and quizzes, to download illustrations and popular songs—Dalida, Hervé Vilard, and my favorite, Alain Souchon. That would add a bit to Younja the Bitch's repertoire, which was limited to Adamo's "Tombe la neige."

When I phoned Salome to put a stop to her messages, she sounded in low spirits.

"How are you, Salome?" I asked.

"Bad, very bad."

"Ah, I'm sorry."

There was a heavy silence. I could detect the sound

of her breathing, a high-pitched rustling, like wind passing through pine needles. I imagined the heat in her room, the sunlight on the drawn curtains, the smell of sweat on her clothes. I felt a pinch in my heart, like something over-familiar but necessary.

"I can come and see you now."

I said the words without really thinking about them. Immediately, I felt the relief that they had brought Salome, like a sigh, or like breathing more easily. It was simple, after all. Any action provokes a reaction. It could even have been a lie, just for the fun of it. Cruel, but lately, I had learned to be cruel. Like Mr. Pak, who would fix a rendezvous then not turn up, or phone without leaving a message. From a phone booth, or a restricted number, that of the bookstore for example. It was no use trying to call him back.

"When?" she asked.

"Now, if you want."

"Take a taxi and keep the receipt, and I'll refund you."

"But I don't have money for a taxi."

"I'll order a taxi. Where are you?"

"At school."

"I'll call the taxi."

One minute later:

"The taxi will be there in fifteen minutes, at the front gate of your campus."

"Okay."

I was struck by the changes that had occurred in Salome's body over the past few weeks. It was as if time, which had passed normally for me, hour after hour, day after day after night, had begun to gallop for her. Her face was still beautiful (I had always thought it resembled a drawing by Dante Gabriel Rossetti, the bridge of her nose a little high, the arches of her brows casting a shadow from which her eyes shone out, and the fringe of black hair cut straight across with scissors), but her expression was strange, slightly rigid, as if something frightening was lying in wait, and she could not free herself of it. She was hunched in her chair, with a blanket over her knees despite the heat.

She greeted me with a forced smile.

"Long time no see," she said.

"Not so long," I started to say.

But she would not listen, she made an impatient gesture.

"I don't want to hear that. I want you to tell me the end of the stories."

Her voice had changed too, there was a veil over her vocal cords. She breathed quickly, her mouth half open, the warm air whistling between her teeth; I thought I could hear the sound of a steam engine, but it was only the inner forge of her lungs at work.

"The presumed assassin?" she asked.

"He's disappeared . . . for the time being."

"What do you mean, disappeared? Those people never disappear completely."

She looked at me. I was about to say something trite, about how the rain made everything disappear, but her eyes prevented me. It looked like she knew something or suspected something I did not understand.

"But I don't need that story," she continued.

I began the ceremony, fetching the little cups and saucers from the sideboard, the teabags, and the Salam teapot her father had brought back from England for her. I pressed down the switch of the kettle, then I waited, standing in front of the window. Through the net curtains I could see the empty street, the cement of the road shiny with rain, and the plants. This square in the wall was all that Salome could see of the world. Even the sky was out of sight, hidden by tall buildings.

"Hurry up!"

It was the first time that Salome had ever given me an order, but her voice belied her words, because it was much more like a complaint, breathed out between her thin lips, trembling on her breath.

I sat down in front of her, not in an armchair, but on the little low chair, a seamstress's chair, which allowed me to be facing her, at her feet, so to speak. It was the pose of the storyteller, I think, and I liked it well enough. I remembered my father's sister, who in fact was his half-sister. We had called her *gomo*, or paternal aunt, and I had thought that was her name. When she told her stories, I would sit on the floor at her feet and let her stroke my hair gently.

The end of the story of Mr. Cho, for Salome

Late August 2016

The truth is, that there is always an end to everything, even to the most incredible stories. Even Mr. Cho knew that. That was why he had so long postponed the moment when he would send off his travelers, his dear Black Dragon and Diamond, to the far side of the earth.

Perhaps deep down he feared the final ordeal. He had been waiting so long for this moment, the return to his native land. He had been waiting since he was a child in Ganghwado Island with his mother, and she sang for him the famous "Arirang" ballad in the evening, her eyes turned towards the line of mist masking the other shore of the wide river. He remembered it well, and he had remembered it almost every night of his life, at the hour when the light faded, like a prayer.

"One day, one day, we will cross the river, we will cross over the mountains, and we will be home again." That was what his mother sang to him, when he was a child, rocking him, so that he fell asleep and dreamed that he was flying across to the other side. Maybe he was the only one to remember it. When he had spoken about it to his wife, Han Seonhee, she made fun of him. At first, gently. "All little boys dream of going to heaven with their mother!" Then, over the years, her mocking became grumpy and embittered. "Well, go and look then, see just how good things are on the other side.

Mr. Cho felt that the time had come. Since his wife's death, he had lived in preparation for this return. Now there was no one to oppose his fantasies. His daughter had grown up, married an office worker in the immigrant service (mostly Chinese immigrants) and had neither the time nor the wish to criticize her father. He could do what he wanted with his pigeons, she did not care.

On the other hand, Mr. Cho was well aware of the need to make the decision while there was time. Although he still felt very vigorous for a retiree —and his job as a janitor in the Good Luck! building left him quite a lot of leisure time—he realized that the years remaining were going to become shorter and shorter. One day he would not have the strength to undertake such a journey.

At the end of the 1960s, the war had been over for a long time, but there were regularly problems at the border. There had been skirmishes between the soldiers of North and South in the DMZ, in Goseong, in Inje. There were no casualties or deaths, but shooting had taken place, with real bullets, and even a few mortar shells. All that could be repeated at any time.

Mr. Cho could not leave anything to chance. He decided on a special training for his birds. He had first thought of setting off firecrackers, like those fired off on New Year's Eve. But the crackling of those little objects seemed ridiculous. It was not a matter of frightening sparrows, but of preparing his pigeons for the greatest and most dangerous journey they would ever undertake.

So he decided to take a bus to the south of the city, to a place close to the zoo, then climb up the winding road through the pine woods. There, in a clearing, was a shooting range. Having looked around, Mr. Cho decided that it was best to position himself a little to the east of the range, on a hillock, in a place where no one could surprise him.

It was still early and the center had only just opened. Shortly before noon Mr. Cho set the pigeons free, first Finch and his wife Vixen, then President and Traveling Girl, then Fly, followed by his wife Cicada. The detonations of pistols and guns echoed in the blue sky, and there was an odor of powder floating in the air. When the firing grew more intense, with the arrival of machine guns and submachine guns, loud and powerful, Mr. Cho delicately seized Black Dragon in the cage, and stroked him for a long time. Black Dragon was his hero, the one who would accomplish the task. Then he launched him towards the sky, in the direction of the firing range, and immediately afterwards, Diamond soared up, drawing a large circle above the pines.

Mr. Cho waited until evening for the birds to return. The firing of rifles in the pine forest had covered all other noises. You could not hear the cars on the nearby motorway, nor the rasp of the cicadas. Mr. Cho was thinking of what his mother must have heard when she ran through the countryside with her baby boy hanging in a shawl behind her back, while bursts of machine gun fire and exploding shells raged, when she staggered through the water of the rice paddies at Pohang-dong in Masan, at the end of the summer, long ago, in 1950. Mr. Cho had only been a small child then, but he felt like he could recognize each explosion, each bullet's hiss, each shock wave of shells exploding in the ground.

Towards dusk, as mist began to cover the sky, Mr. Cho saw the birds. They were circling, two couples separated by only a few wing-spans, seeking their master. The machine guns had fallen silent. The cicadas had resumed their concert, in waves, rising and falling in tune with the noise of the cars on the road.

Mr. Cho gave the signal, clapping his hands, and the pigeons approached, first the females, then the two males, landing on the dry ground in the midst of the pines. They had been flying all day but did not seem tired. When Mr. Cho took them in his hands, he felt that their little hearts were still beating rapidly, from the excitement of this long day of freedom above the hills. Mr. Cho put them back, one after the other, into the cages, without feeding them, just a little water in the beakers attached to the bars. He himself had eaten nothing and drunk nothing all day long, as if to accompany the pigeons in their ordeal. He felt a great pride, because his creatures had survived, and now nothing could stand in the way of the success of their return journey to the native land.

Salome had stretched out a little on her chair, without moving her arms and legs, just slightly relaxing her muscles. The expression of anguish had disappeared from her face. She was almost smiling.

"So when are they going to leave for good?" she asked.

"Tomorrow," I said. I could have said at once, but the daylight had faded outside as in the story, the rain had stopped, and I decided that it would be tomorrow for her, for me, and for Mr. Cho.

Tomorrow duly arrived.

This is the big day for Mr. Cho, the day of departure. He has hired the services of a market van, and set out with his pigeons on their last adventure, on the other side of the border. He knows the place well. It's where he grew up with his mother, when they came back from farther south after the war, in 1956. It's the closest place to where he was born, just on the other side of the estuary of the Hangang River. His mother wanted to settle in this isolated village, because that way she felt like she would be able to communicate with the members of her family who had stayed behind, with her lost husband, her grandfather, with all that she had lost. She sometimes spoke to her son about the old life, when they lived on the pear farm and lacked nothing. She did not talk much about his father. He had been a farmhand, but also a handsome man, tall and strong, with a fine voice, a singer of popular ballads, and that was how he had seduced her and given her a child, but her family had looked down on him. When the war broke out, he ran away to join the Northern troops and she never heard from him again. So she chose to leave with the child. She crossed the river on a raft and then traveled southward to Pohang-dong. Now the memories come back to Mr. Cho, especially the song of "Arirang," and his eyes fill with tears as he opens the cages of the birds one after the other.

"Off you go. Fly high up into the sky, go to my native land, to the farm buried in the hollow in the mountains. You'll recognize it, thanks to the beautiful plantations of flowering pear trees; you will carry my letters to my family, to my nephews and my nieces, to my cousins, you will tell them that I am still alive, you will give them the words I wrote for them, down here, on the other side of the river, words of hope and love, words of joy and laughter, words of happiness!"

Salome closed her eyes in the warm, soft afternoon light. She listened to Mr. Cho's words, to the sound of the wind in the wings of the birds, the rustle of their feathers, the wind that raised them above the dark water of the great river, the ripples that trembled on the water as on the skin of an animal, the smell of the approaching earth, the sounds of the fields, the shouting voices, the laughter of children.

"Listen," I continued. "The wind comes from the sea, the clear wind of morning. Breathe in and feel the wind on the skin of your face, Salome, as you fly aloft in the sky, northwards to the other side of the world. This is your last journey, with Black Dragon, with Diamond, with the others. The wind intoxicates you, the wind dazzles your eyes and takes your breath away, but you continue to fly, you are heading straight toward the end of your journey, you stretch out your arms and you feel the wind on your body. You do not weigh anything now, you're a feather in the wind, a leaf, a petal, and below you the river with its islands pushes you upwards, northwards, to the country of return."

Salome kept her eyes shut, while I spoke more and more quietly, more and more slowly. She opened her hands, she felt the air between her fingers, she breathed in the wind, she tasted the salt of the sea and the honey of the flowering meadows, the long stems of the reeds waving in the wind, the foliage of the trees, the shining hedges of camellias, and all the roads that intersected—not roads, but paths lined with stone walls—and the blue roofs of villages. The words transported her. She did not even need to hear them. They were born in her mind like rockets taking off.

The pigeons flew on all day long, until nightfall, over valleys and hills, over yellow rice fields and rapeseed fields, over factories and yards, over the gray villages, airfields, lakes, and rivers, and when the night arrived, they recognize the place where their master was born, the narrow valley sunk between two mountains, where the fruit trees grow. After a final circle in the sky, they landed on the roofs of the buildings, one couple, then another, and another; they were all there, none was missing, none was lost. As they walked over the roof of the barn, their claws scratched the metal, and in their throats began the cooing of peace, their little song, sweet and sad, their love greeting before mating.

I seemed to be there, too. I closed my eyes, I heard the voices of the people living on the farm.

First the cries of the children, who, spotting the pigeons on the roof of the barn, cry "Ho-ho-ho!" Then the adults, who came out one after another, the women in aprons, the men with sunburnt faces. They were tall. They had powerful shoulders, hardened hands. They all stopped in front of the cement-block house and looked up at the birds they had never seen before. Then one of them placed a ladder against the wall, climbed up slowly, cautiously, and seized Black Dragon. The bird let himself be seized. He was so tired after the journey that he could not even struggle. On the ground, everyone surrounded the bird, and at that moment Diamond flew down in turn, with a rustle of wings, and took her place beside her mate, and then the other pairs came down, one after another, and the children took them into their hands, laughing. It was at that moment that a little girl named Misun exclaimed, "Look, there's a letter attached to its leg!" She pointed at the little scroll of paper, which the man unrolled and the woman deciphered in a loud voice, just one word: *Future*.

It was a secret word, and leapt from mouth to mouth, while the other papers were unrolled, one after another, with their one-word messages. Someone said the word "spy," a frightening word, and everyone took a step back, but the pigeons only quietly pecked at the grains of rice that Misun had brought out. It was the middle of the day. The winter sun pierced the mist. The pigeons had arrived, guided by a mysterious and evident order, and they spoke of the other world, on the other side of the river estuary, a world that thus ceased to be foreign. They walked on the ground, amidst the inhabitants of the great collective farm of pear trees that would bloom when spring came. This was the end of their journey. Tomorrow or in a few days, maybe, Misun and the children would write a word on a sheet of paper, and wrap it around the right leg of Black Dragon, and so with all the pigeons, just a word, such as "felicity," or "love," or "happiness," then they would take the birds in their hands and launch them into the sky, in the direction of their return."

Salome leaned back in her chair, her head tilted a little to one side. Her eyes were full of tears, but I did not know if they were tears of joy or of distress. This was the end of a story, the end of a journey.

I took her hand and held it for a long time. Her hand was warm and dry, feverish.

I left gently, without saying goodbye. It was time for her treatment. The nurse was standing in front of the door of the drawing-room, her white apron shining in the darkness, like an apparition. Mr. Cho realized his dream. He was back. He no longer wanted anything else, for to him the world was perfect. But here, but for us who lived elsewhere, nothing was really finished. Happiness did not exist. Just a few dreams, a few words. Just the sea breeze that ruffled the feathers of birds as they cross the estuary.

And a deadly reality.

The rainy season left us weary, Salome and I, as if all that water flowing in the streets and evaporating on the overheated cement of the roads had washed us and scoured us, twisted us and thrown us away, emptied of strength.

I decided to move once more. The room in the basement had become far too unhealthy. The rain brought out suspicious stains on the walls, and the big rat that had given up invading my space for a moment had come back full of strength. Assisted by some friends, it would push every night against the zinc plate I had screwed into the wall, and I distinctly heard the grinding of its teeth. It seemed to me that it had digested the dough made of rice flour and crushed glass and now had come back to make me hear, as a reproach, the sound of its teeth crushing the last crumbs of glass, a phantom sound. I also saw cockroaches running about in the bathroom (actually just a showerhead suspended above a squat toilet), and as the saying goes, when you see one rat, there are ten, and when you see one cockroach, there are a hundred. I did not want to count them.

Thanks to a friend of my mother, I obtained the address of a house to rent at the other end of the city, far to the south. In fact, I didn't even know if it was part of the city or part of the countryside. It took more than an hour on the subway to reach the station, Oryu-dong. I prepared my suitcase, my purse, and my backpack, into which I had stuffed all my things, sheets, clothes, and even a little pillow in the form of a rabbit that my mother had given me when I left our village in Jeolla-do. I set off early in the morning, before the neighborhood was awake, so as not to risk being seen by the owner, to whom I owed three months' rent, or by the terrible stalker (although he had totally disappeared since the rainy season— maybe he had melted like a snowman in the sun). I left without leaving any address or any regrets. The time I spent in the neighborhood I called El Sordido had been the worst months of my life.

I liked the new neighborhood because it looked a little like the streets of my village back home, ugly and straight, without any fancy shops, but without rats either. The brick building was on the edge of an avenue covered with tiny, stunted trees. I had an apartment on the second floor above a cold noodle restaurant, and the owner, a lady named Ahn Soyoung, presented that as an advantage.

"At any hour of the day, and even at night, you can go down and give my name, and they will give you something to eat, and it will cost you almost nothing."

Whereas in El Sordido I had known no one, avoiding the neighbors and especially the landlord, who was always greedy for cash, in Oryu-dong I had good neighbors, and even friends, at once. They were modest people for the most part, except for my upstairs neighbor who was a math teacher in a college next to Sungkonghoe University. There was a shoe-maker whose shop was in a metal container installed near the bridge, women working as housekeepers in service apartments, mothers of families, small officials in the government offices in Sindorim or Yeongdeungpo. As people would leave early for their work, and the mothers accompanied their children to school, the mornings were very calm, and I could sleep until noon. (I always loved sleeping late; it was one of the things I quarreled with my father about, because to go to the fish market it was necessary to get up before dawn).

I also liked my new subway station. After crossing the bridge over the river, the train stopped above ground at Dangsan Station on Line 2, and then passed below neighborhoods with large buildings, and little by little more popular neighborhoods, filled with houses with three floors poorly built, tightly clustered together. From Sindorim, Line 1 took me to Oryu-dong Station, and once the train emerged into the open air, I could see the different districts, all with very different, modern buildings, large parks, busy streets, then again small brick houses with sheet roofs, all the way to Oryu-dong. I had to go down the stairs and pass under the lines, and I liked this great crossroads with all these avenues, and the bolted iron bridge. I felt I was traveling somewhere in America. I imagined the bridge in Oryu-dong resembling Brooklyn Bridge, and the avenues and streets in my neighborhood resembling those of the popular neighborhoods of New York, the Bronx, or Queens. Even the name Oryu pleased me. It sounded like it would be the name of a Tokyo neighborhood (another capital I would love to know).

I quickly established some habits. I felt, for the first time, very free. I had no one I needed to give account to, and I was far away from my aunt and her delightful Baekhwa. There was no risk of them visiting me. For my elementary French course at Hongik University, I managed to negotiate an arrangement with Younja, my exploiter. I would continue to take charge of the early morning classes, but on those days, I could spend the night in her office. She hesitated initially, because it was not exactly authorized by the administration, but the office security guard retired early anyway to watch soap operas in bed, and after nine o'clock I had the building to myself. That allowed me to shower and use the toilets without running into anyone. I bought a thin mattress at the market in Seodaemun, which I folded up every morning and put in Younja's cupboard. For food, the small kitchen at the end of the corridor held a microwave and a kettle. That was all I needed to eat my *ramyeon* and drink my coffee in the morning before classes (*ramyeon* is terrible because of the spices and salt, but it's what poor students eat). All this worked out perfectly, and that is why I could say that I had never felt so free in my life.

I enjoyed teaching French. Most of the students (female students I should say, because in the group of eighteen, there was only one boy, and he was a bit effeminate too) had registered for the extra credits. Their actual majors were maths, natural sciences, physics, or even philosophy. I was working with a textbook called *La Joie de Lire*—a title for kindergarteners, actually, not the university level. There were also grammar exercises, and translations of theoretical texts, perfectly unintelligible. One after another, each student had to read the texts in a droning voice, then modify the tense of the verbs, and put the sentences into the interrogative, the negative, and the negative interrogative.

It seems to me that the boat is heading towards the island.

It does not seem to me that the boat is heading towards the island.

The boat, it seems to me, is heading towards the island?

Does it not seem to me that the boat is heading towards the island?

While the students worked on syntax problems, I indulged in sweet reveries on the words, something I always liked doing. I imagined, for example, a boat on the Hangang River slowly gliding over the water, without a motor, just guided by a man at the back with a very long oar, noiselessly approaching the island with flocks of ducks (it was my favorite island on the river), with the tranquil shimmering of the water tracing his movements, bubbles at times rising from the depths and bursting, and I thought of the boat on which the mother of Mr. Cho Hansu had crossed the river with her baby and pigeons, more than fifty years before. The ducks had probably already been there. They would not have fled the bombing. For them an airplane, a truck, and a motor boat were probably all the same.

It was during classes, in the moments of silence, or when the students were reading texts with forced voices, trying unsuccessfully to reproduce the sounds of a language in which p and b are pronounced differently, or the words change in the plural, where it is necessary to place the tongue in the mouth just beneath the internal orifices of the nose to pronounce the extraordinarily nasal sounds—that I began to compose a new story in my head, which I would soon bring to Salome, to see her open her eyes, hear her breathe more strongly. That was how I invented Nabi the singer.

The story of Nabi the singer, for Salome

September 2016

She arrived in Seoul when she was still very young, aged fourteen I think she was, a pretty girl from Gangwon-do province, from a small town called Yeongwol. Her name was Kwon Hyangsu, which meant "perfume water," but also "nostalgia." She had never loved anything other than singing, ever since she was a child. She accompanied her grandmother to church, and very soon she had joined the choir, singing religious hymns, clapping and swinging her hips, which pleased the faithful, especially the boys, but much less her grandmother, an elderly lady of the old school, very strict and authoritarian.

"Don't wriggle about like that while you're singing. You know that the devil is everywhere, even in the house of God."

But Hyangsu would not listen. Every time a hymn began, she could feel the music entering into her, weaving about in her body, and only then did her voice become powerful and clear, dominating all the others, until she was the only one singing before the microphone, and the faithful accompanied her by beating the rhythm in their hands, and the pastor himself pulled back a bit from his piano to listen and watch.

Hyangsu was pretty, but not very tall, so that at the age of fourteen she seemed to be only twelve, even if her breasts were already budding inside her blouse. She liked to wear pretty dresses that showed off her legs with their bouncing calves. She had learned to walk leaning back slightly, because she had read in a magazine that it highlighted her behind and gave the illusion that she was taller. At the church, Pastor Randall (this was not his real name, but he had lived in the United States and had adopted this nickname) often greeted her with the remark, "Here's the girl with pretty legs!" Her grandmother did not like that, but she dared not say anything, because a pastor is a pastor, after all, and Randall was married to a woman a little older than himself, with gray hair and a big rump, and no one would have allowed themselves to criticize such a woman. It was said that she was the one who was really in charge at the church, that she even composed her husband's sermons.

The church occupied a kind of large workshop on

the ground floor of a modern building. Its double doors were more like the entrance to a garage or a nightclub. Beyond the door, there was a four-hundred-seat room with a stage and a cinema screen. It was there that every Sunday Hyangsu went to sing. The choir consisted of six boys and six girls, dressed in blue and white, and only Hyangsu was entitled to come on stage dressed in her pretty dress, or sometimes in jeans with a white shirt, because she was the star of the show. She sang the hymns in Korean, and also in English, to jazzy melodies, and often Randall left his piano and a young boy came on with an electric guitar and accompanied Hyangsu's solos with an R&B rhythm.

Hyangsu lived only for these moments. As she climbed onto the stage, she felt she was someone else, someone very different, a woman, no longer a child, and a woman who knew what she wanted, who led others, who knew how to command respect. When she had finished singing, the congregation would applaud, and that too annoyed her grandmother, who said, "We shouldn't forget where we are. It's not a night club, after all!"

Hyangsu's grandmother had little esteem for Pastor Randall. Everyone knew that he was a worthless man, that he had received the office of pastor by suborning the old pastor, a worthy but naive old man, and that he had given money to win the votes of influential members of the community, especially old widows and wealthy women who were sensitive to his charms and gifts.

Hyangsu's grandmother was severe, but she was generous toward her granddaughter. She tried to redeem the faults committed by Hyangsu's mother, who had abandoned her husband and daughter and run away with another man. Hyangsu's father was also in his own way a good-for-nothing, a womanizer and a liar who was so unscrupulous that he even stole money from the church to go gambling or to buy perfume for his little girlfriends of the moment. But Hyangsu's grandmother indulged him, because he was her youngest son and her last child. She had therefore transferred her love to her granddaughter and the affairs of the church, and the fact that Hyangsu's pretty voice and legs attracted new members for the church did not displease her. On the contrary, she said that everything should contribute to the service of the Lord Jesus.

At the time, Hyangsu was living in her grand-mother's house, with an aunt and her husband, a nervous, nasty little man, but everyone was under the old lady's thumb, and it seemed that everything was normal in this family. Even Jiseok, Hyangsu's father—he was often called Jipye, or literally, "hard cash," a fitting nickname in light of his fondness for gambling —could give the illusion of a normal and regular life. Every morning, everyone had breakfast together in a room adjacent to the church, and Hyangsu's grandmother gave instructions to everyone. Then Hyangsu left for the neighboring school, where she was struggling to complete her schooling. She did not dislike school, but what was talked about there, what her classmates talked about, seemed to her very far from her own life. They talked about shopping, makeup, meeting boys, sports competi-tions, and TV shows. At Hyangsu's grandmother's there was a television, but it served exclusively to project Christian videos. The greatest fantasy that Hyangsu had seen—and she had adored it—was *The Chronicles of Narnia* series, because her grandmother had explained to her the message of the story, the Lion that represents the Lord Jesus, and the battles that the true Christians must engage in if they are to succeed in finding the right way among the impious.

It was at this time that Hyangsu experienced the greatest fortune of her life, one that would finally orient her towards a singing career. Fate struck in the form of a letter from a group of producers looking for candidates for a recording of songs with religious themes, and Pastor Randall summoned Hyangsu to his office. He had not spoken to anyone else, but if she was willing, Hyangsu might well be the singer that this production company was looking for. The girl felt her heart beat faster. What Randall said was what she had long hoped for without believing, that one day her time would come, and that she would be able to give herself entirely to what she loved in life. But at the same time, she hesitated. Would her grandmother agree? Singing in a choir for the faithful, in church, was one thing, but singing for producers, to make money, was very different. She stood before the great man, her hands clasped behind her back, with her fingers crossed to force destiny. She did not know what to say. She felt herself blushing, and she was ashamed that he should see that.

The audition was held the following day, at the Jericho production headquarters, at the far end of the city. Hyangsu went there by subway, and at the entrance to the building she glimpsed Pastor Randall in the middle of a small group of people. An elegant woman, slightly snobbish-looking, accompanied her to the recording studio. For the test, with the agreement of Randall, they had chosen a song in English, one that Hyangsu hardly knew but had heard on the radio. The words went:

King of all days
Oh so highly exalted
Glorious in heaven above

Here I am to worship
Here I am to bow down . . .

Hyangsu took a deep breath, arched her back, and began to sing unaccompanied in a somewhat grave voice. Then the rhythm of the music took hold of her, and she began to sway, singing, eyes closed, as if she were in front of a crowd, on the stage in the church,

Here I am to worship
Here I am to bow down . . .

When she had finished, she opened her eyes. The technicians, the elegant woman, even Randall, were all looking at her, and she understood in their eyes that she had been hired. She was trembling so much that she had to lean on the pastor's arm as she left after signing the contracts. It was as if she had just been reborn into a new world, under a new sun. She was eager to announce the news to her grandmother. But when she told her about the contract she had signed, her grandmother objected.

"How can a sixteen-year-old girl sign a thing like that? It's ridiculous. You should tear up the paper and forget about it."

The weeks that followed were difficult for Hyangsu. She did not dare beg her grandmother, but the idea of a new life as a singer spun in her head day and night, especially at night, until she was dizzy.

Randall decided to make the austere old lady change her mind.

"It's for religion, not for fun," he said. "It's a gift

from heaven, no one has the right to reject it."

Finally, the grandmother gave in. Hyangsu could record, two or three times a week, on condition that it did not get in the way of her duties as a Christian or of her studies. That day, Randall summoned Hyangsu to his office to announce the good news. It was a weekday, a little before noon, an hour when nobody was around in the building. Hyangsu went to the meeting with a pounding heart, because the pastor had already hinted that he had obtained her grandmother's consent, so she could continue with the recordings and become the star singer at Jericho. But she could not foresee the trap that the man had prepared for her.

"Come closer, young lady," Randall told her when she entered. The office was overheated by the midday sun, and the red curtains were drawn over the window. There was a kind of exciting half-light filling the silence of the closed church. Hyangsu listened to the sound her heart made in her chest, and her hands remained clenched behind her back.

"Come closer, you mustn't be afraid of me. We've known each other for a long time now, haven't we?"

Why was he speaking like that? His voice was

strange. It was not the stentorian voice with which Pastor Randall harangued the faithful every Sunday, nor the soft, rather syrupy voice with which he sang the sacred songs, stressing the *a*'s and the *o*'s or making the *ch* and *k* syllables sound too strong. His whispering voice was slightly shrill, emerging from between his clenched teeth, as if he were murmuring a secret. Hyangsu listened and could not move, let alone approach the desk as the pastor was telling her to, but she was also unable to step back. She felt that her feet were fixed to the ground, screwed to the wooden floor of the office. She stood there, barely breathing, her eyes lowered, awaiting what would come next, and would inevitably come, like in a bad dream.

"Hyangsu, Hyangsu. I think of you all the time. You're my little girl with the pretty legs, the girl that lights up my nights. Do you realize that?"

Pastor Randall had not left his desk, but his large body had begun to lean forward. He gradually slipped from his chair and now was only a few inches away from Hyangsu. She felt it without really seeing. It seemed to her that this man, usually so stiff and distant, had become like a serpent, sliding and twisting over the tabletop. His face approached her belly, her breasts. She felt on her dress, on her bodice, the warmth of his breath while he continued to speak, though she could not hear what he was saying, merely the hissing of words repeating the same things, the whistling of her first name, spoken in low, insistent tones, with sighs and silences.

"Pretty legs, pretty legs," said the voice, and Hyangsu wondered if he was talking about her, about her legs, her body. Now she looked at him and saw little drops of sweat beading on his forehead, where the hair had receded, and over his bushy eyebrows. She saw the tops of his eyelids, somewhat gray and wrinkled, and the rest of his body, the white shirt crumpled at the collar, the arms leaning on the table, and the hands advancing, two dark, muscular animals, traversed on the backs by veins in the shape of tree branches. The hands that clasped her legs, then slowly slid upwards, towards the forbidden places.

I stopped. I looked at Salome. Her head was leaning a little to one side, as if her neck did not have enough strength to hold it straight. The skin of her face was ashen, her eyelids closed. When I stopped talking, she opened her eyes and looked at me. I did not know what I should read in her eyes. Was it fear, or anger? What had she been thinking? That I was going to tell her fairy tales, invent a blue country, a princess? When my aunt Migyeong used to tell me stories of ghouls and werewolves, *gwisin* ghosts and witches, all the time stroking my hair, I had felt a delicious shiver, as if I were looking through a forbidden door and could see a dark, malevolent world very near the surface of life, within reach of my hand. This was the world that I wanted to give to Salome.

"Tell me what happened next, please, *eonni*!"

Salome called me *eonni*, her elder sister, as I had with my aunt Migyeong, in a somewhat plaintive little girl's voice, and I understand at once that now, dependent as she was on my words and my dreams, she had become my younger sister, my creature. I did not know why, but this discovery, which should have satisfied me, troubled me rather more than was right. I felt a kind of vertigo. The roles were suddenly reversed. I, her servant, her employee, paid in bills of 50,000 won adorned with the effigy of the worthy old lady, had become her mistress, one she must follow blindly through the meanderings of the imagination, at the mercy of my words and desires. I had the power to continue or interrupt the flow which added time to her life and delayed the hour of her death.

The light was fading on the red curtains drawn against the sunlight, which Salome could no longer look at because of her illness. When she complained of the pain that the light caused at the back of her eyes, I bought her some blue-tinted glasses from a fashion store around Ewha Womans University. She tried them on, then placed them on the table beside her, and now they had disappeared. She hadn't mentioned them since, but I understood that she didn't want any disguises. She wanted to face her problems on her own.

What happened that day in Pastor Randall's office was the beginning of a new life for Hyangsu. She did not tell anyone, especially not her grandmother, but from that moment she stopped attending church. She did not explain. When her grandmother told her, "Hyangsu, dear, your place is in the choir," she did not reply, just looked away, and in her eyes, there was something sad and closed that kept her grandmother from insisting.

Then she started hanging out with a group of musicians, boys older than herself, who played rock in clubs at night, and she became their singer. The bass guitarist, a tall boy named David Choi, told her, "If you're going to be part of the band, you'll have to find a name for yourself." She liked the idea, since she no longer wanted to keep her little girl's name, so she chose *Nabi*, Butterfly. She had initially thought of calling herself *Mudangbeolle*, or Ladybug, because she liked the little creatures with their red and black spots that sometimes landed on her hand before flying straight up into the air on some secret mission. But Nabi was on the shorter side. And she also realized that ladybugs were fragile and could easily be trapped by spiders. Gummy, meaning Spider, was the stage name of Hyangsu's favorite singer. So, from then on, she was, and would always be, Nabi.

I was tired of telling stories, and Salome was tired of listening. I could see that from her heavy gaze, her ashen eyelids. There would be no tea this time. I did not have the strength to put the water on to boil, wait, then pour the water onto the paper teabags in the Salam teapot. Maybe Nabi's story was eating up our energy. Maybe it was one of those stories the end of which we did not want to hear.

I left without saying goodbye, without greeting the nurse sitting in the kitchen, who was tapping on her phone. Was everything all too predictable, hopeless? Then so was the life of Salome, or at least what remained to be lived of her life. My doctor friend Yuri, who was finishing up her studies in epidemic pathology as an intern at a major hospital, had told me Salome's disease was an incurable, incomprehensible sickness that, little by little, shut down the vital forces, like the very slow fading of a flower. All the functions faded away, day after day, one sleepless night after another, except for the brain—the imagination, the anxiety, and the longing to be happy, or perhaps the grudges, the jealousies, the diabolical conspiracies. You became like a spaceship lost in the cosmic immensities. Your head no longer commanded anything, but only assisted in your shipwreck.

"It's not a disease, Bitna," Yuri had said. "It's a curse."

The word astonished me, but I understood. Yuri was very religious, a Latter-day Saint, as they are called. She knew the story of Job lying on his dung heap, devoured by a nameless sickness, because God wanted it.

I, too, know that we must humble ourselves, recognize that we are nothing at all, renounce revolt and life itself.

But I am more on the side of the Buddhists, even though I do not really believe in reincarnation. I believe that life is an ocean that bathes us all, and that death carries us all together toward another form that we know nothing of. I also believe that we are all bound to one another, children with parents, parents with their offspring, and that those not yet born touch those who are alive today and reach out a hand to those who are no more.

"*Eonni*, I was so afraid you would not come back."

Salome tried to stand up from her chair. The cushion that supported her back slid down, and in trying to catch it, she lost control of the tartan blanket that had been covering her despite the stifling, post-typhoon heat. I saw her legs, two very white, very thin limbs tucked up under her, in the position of a jockey spurring on an invisible horse. I put the blanket back very gently, with the gestures of an older sister, and I saw Salome's hand rise from the armrest, trying to touch my face, to stroke my hair.

"We're going to finish this story about Nabi, because it's really too sad!"

She said this in a falsely playful tone, which was contradicted by the sound of her voice, tight with anguish.

I replied in the same tone, "Yes, let's finish, then I can end with the story of the wannabe murderer, and also the two dragons."

Salome clapped. "Yes, yes, please, I love fantastic tales!"

Had Salome given the nurse a lecture? Mrs. Wang (such was her royal family name, that of the Korean kings in an earlier dynasty) made her entrance into the living room carrying a tray with the Salam teapot, cups, and cookies from a Tous les Jours bakery. How did Salome guess that I was low on money and hadn't eaten since the day before? Perhaps, with the cunning familiar to people who suffer, she realized why I had returned today to finish the story begun only yesterday, and receive my fee in beautiful, crisp 50,000-won bills.

Nabi was now living a life different from anything she had ever experienced. One day, she left her grandmother's house without warning. She climbed out through the ground-floor window and found herself in the street, without luggage, without money. She went to live in the boys' recording studio, where she had been invited by David Choi, in the basement of a building in the southern part of town, in the small streets around Gyodae Station. The boys bought her a mattress and pushed the furniture and electronic devices against the wall. There was a sink and toilet on the landing. It was warm and silent like a cocoon.

Every evening, Nabi woke up and let the boys in. They played their instruments and Nabi sang the songs they had written. Then she added words and tunes, so that now they were playing her songs. These were her favorite moments, when the sound of music invaded the little studio, colliding with the walls and the ceiling, seeking to escape, and she sang, sometimes shouting, sometimes in a low, husky voice. David told her she had a deep, sexy voice. He wanted Nabi to move around a bit while she is singing, because that was what was expected from a rock singer, but Nabi stood still, shoulders well back. Her uniform was jeans and a white shirt, and now the boys had adopted that, too. They had exchanged their shorts and Bermudas and fancy T-shirts for black jeans and long-sleeved white shirts. They changed their name too. They were no longer the Flamines, or Dexter, or the Intros, or even Black Jeans White Shirt. They were called NABI. They had simply adopted her name. They played for her, and they lived for her.

Salome liked this moment of the story. Her eyes lit up, she smiled a painful smile, trying to imagine the small studio, the music exploding, the sounds of the percussion beating against the walls, and little Hyangsu motionless in the center of the room, her black hair shining under the glow of the naked light bulb in the ceiling, and her low voice, louder than the music, spelling out the words, inconsequential words, free words, words stronger than acts, stronger than death . . .

After that, things progressed very quickly for Nabi and the boys. The legend of the Jericho singer had already circulated online, and the boys contacted producers, organized private evenings, concerts in the Gangnam clubs, performances at public festivals, on the stage in front of the Sinchon Station shopping center, and in Incheon. A photographer became interested in her, a man of a certain age named Namgil, a bit eccentric, who owned a studio called Pearl Underground in Yeouido. He transformed his studio for her, into an aviary (of course, it was the name Nabi that inspired him), with birds of all colors flying freely between branches of magnolias in pots and even some butterflies. Nabi had never imagined anything like it. She had the impression of experiencing a waking dream. The pictures Namgil took were amazing, her face enlarged to the size of a whole wall, her eyes with their dilated pupils seeming to reflect a sea (to enlarge her pupils he gave Nabi a strange beverage, made of a decoction of red Datura flowers, and her dreams continued long after the photo session was over). And Namgil was very soft and slightly plump, like a big cat, or like a teddy bear. Nabi coiled up in his arms to sleep all afternoon, while he whispered nice things in her ear. It was the first time in a long time that there had been any tenderness in her life, since the evenings spent in the company of her aunt, listening to her stories of witches and werewolves.

Salome listened attentively to every word, as if it were her own story. She knew very well that I was not inventing anything. I never knew how to invent, just change names, imagine places. But of course she could not know that I too had an aunt who was an expert in the art of scaring little children.

She said, "Was this photographer, Namgil, a good friend?"

"No, of course not," I replied. "He was a wolf, like the others, like Randall. Nabi fell prey to him, as she would to the stalker. You know the words of the Bible, like a lamb thrown to the wolves. Her grandmother did not want her to start a career as a singer, far from the church. She knew very well what awaited her, but she couldn't stop it. Now Nabi must go to the end of what she has chosen."

Salome seemed to shudder at my words. For her, I know, the stories were not just stories, they were also sensations that touched her, burned her skin, feeling like needles stuck into her knuckles, waves of pain behind her eyes. She demanded them, and she suffered because of them, she feared them. It seemed to me that I could hear the beating of her heart through the skin of her forearms. I see the pulsations in her exposed neck, at the level of the jugular vein.

But I had to go on, no matter what, even if every story I told Salome robbed her of a moment of life.

So Hyangsu grew famous under the name Nabi, and she became the mistress of the photographer Namgil. That did not please the boys, because they were all in love with her, even if with them it had never gone beyond flirting in between concerts, once with one, once with the other, or sometimes with all three at the same time, in the clubs at night, with the heat and the spotlights like electric thunderstorms. With Namgil, it was calmer. It happened the first time in his studio, among the climbing plants and birds. He unfastened her bodice, he kissed her on the breasts, and they made love very gently. She did not enjoy it but she liked the proximity of his body, the musky smell of his skin, and his long hair, which he untied so that it hid his face.

Next, Nabi's pictures were published in magazines, first in Seoul, then in the United States, in *Vogue*, in *Esquire*, even in *Forbes*, and then almost at the same time, all over the world, in Mexico, England, and France. Now her agent had no need to negotiate primetime spots, it was she who was invited, who was the main lead, the top of the bill, and Namgil fired the agent. He became her producer, her protector, maybe also her profiteer, or that was what the boys claimed. They soon felt their pain when they were sacked too, replaced by musicians chosen for each concert by Namgil, no longer amateurs, or kids, but real musicians, seasoned, recognized, with sound technicians who had worked in Los Angeles and New York, not in a small cellar soundproofed with egg cartons somewhere in Seoul.

Now, it was no longer Nabi who wrote her songs. She had tried to, but Namgil remained intractable.

"Nabi, baby," he said to her, and he never spoke loudly, he remained very soft, he caressed the girl's hair as if he were her *oppa*, her older brother, not her lover. "I know what's good for you. The time of lullabies is over. Now you have to start your real life. You're a great singer. You're going to go all over the world, you're going to fill the halls in London, New York, Tokyo, and everyone will follow you, everyone will love you. What revenge for you, the little girl without a mother, who had to sing in churches, who was mistreated, despised, who ran away from home to escape misfortune."

As he spoke, Nabi felt tears overflowing from her eyes and running down her cheeks. It was the first time she had felt the sadness that was rooted in her heart, that blocked her throat and tied knots in her stomach. The soft voice of Namgil entered her and untied the knots one by one, releasing the water that was in her memory, and the water overflowed from under her eyelids.

What the photographer had said was the truth. Now Nabi had no more free time. Every day she was preparing singing tours, she was recording CDs, she was on the radio or on TV. She could no longer live just anywhere, as she had done until then. Namgil found her an apartment in a large building not far from the river, on the thirteenth floor, which he had summarily furnished with a mattress and plastic sofas, and a large television screen. The interest of the building lay in its anonymity. No one cared about anyone else, and the entrance was protected by a code and especially by a security guard, a retired policeman capable of deterring intruders and the curious. The guard immediately became friendly toward Nabi. He greeted her politely when she came in and went out, and she replied with a charming smile. She felt free and happy for the first time in her life, with the music in her heart and the care shown her by the photographer. She felt like a little pampered animal, a sort of sweet and dreamy doll, sometimes sitting for hours on the mattress in front of the big window, watching the river shine in the distance. Sometimes she thought of her past, and missed the old days, especially the company of the three boys. She did not often hear from them. Sometimes they were waiting for her at the end of a concert, on the curb, with the crowd of hysterical little girls shouting when Nabi passed by. They tried to talk to her, but the bodyguards pushed them away, and the photographer took Nabi by the arm and dragged her towards the limo parked along the sidewalk. What did they want to say? She had not the faintest idea, but it made her a little nervous, as if they were messengers from her previous life, who knew something she did not know, as if they wanted to warn her of danger.

Once, she talked about it with Namgil, but he dismissed the idea with an abrupt gesture.

"Don't think about any of that, Nabi, they don't matter anymore, and I'll even tell you, they're jealous of your success, and your money. They probably want you to share it with them. I happen to know that they once thought of hiring a lawyer to claim their rights. That's why I told you not to sing the old songs. They're greedy, they want to suck your blood!"

This news troubled Nabi a lot. She could not believe that the boys who had helped her and who had been so kind to her could have changed so much in just a few years. All of a sudden, she felt very lonely in life, alone despite the crowds that came to hear her sing, despite meetings with reporters and producers, despite the little gifts and attentions of Namgil. The only person with whom she had a normal relationship was the old policeman who lived at the entrance of the building in a small room under the stairs. She did not know his name, but sometimes she came down at the end of the day when she had a free moment, and she stayed and talked to him.

He would talk about his life, about life after the war, about his mother who had crossed the river beneath the bombs, carrying him on her back. He even showed her a photo he had found on the Internet, taken by an American soldier, showing a young woman dressed in rags like a beggar, packets of rags at her feet and, tied to her back in a large shawl, a little baby with eyes enlarged by hunger and fear, his head shaved, his nose filthy with snot, and his mouth black with dust.

"Look, it's me with my mum, after we crossed the 38th parallel. We were heading south."

Attached to the packets there was also a little bag pierced with holes, in which were enclosed two homing pigeons, but he did not mention that.

Behind the woman was a devastated landscape, pitted with bomb craters. And the great river, which Nabi recognized at once. She was not sure that the guardian of the building was telling the truth, that it was really him and his mom in the photo, but it troubled her, and later, when she thought about it, she had tears in her eyes, because it made her think of her own mother, who had abandoned her when she was a baby, to go and live with another man.

Salome listened quietly. Maybe she was also moved, because it was her story, too, in a way. Her father and mother had decided to commit suicide, leaving all their possessions to their daughter, in order to escape from incurable disease. And now it was her turn to be sick, with death at the end of the road, very close.

Someone else came into Nabi's life. One day, Namgil introduced her to a woman whose name was Kim Yumi. She was twenty-three years old, with a rather long face and very smooth black hair that reached the small of her back. She was to be Nabi's secretary. She would prepare meetings with the press, she would keep her diary. She spoke softly, with a kind of shyness. She always stayed a little to one side, behind Namgil. After a short time, she became indispensable to Nabi, the only person between her and the rest of the world. She became a friend. Between concerts she would stay with Nabi for part of the day, accompany her to a restaurant, or go shopping with her. She did not talk much but just listened to Nabi.

At first, she called her *seonsaengnim,* as if Nabi

were older than herself.

Nabi protested, "Call me *eonni* instead, if you want, but I am not your mistress."

To try to help her, Nabi called her *yeodongsaeng*, or little sister, but still Yumi could only respond with Hyangsu-*ssi*, Miss Hyangsu. With Yumi's arrival, life had changed. Nabi no longer spent so much time sitting on her mattress looking out of the window. She would wait for Yumi's phone call to go out, and they would take the taxi together, going to the mall, or eating a snack lunch at the little restaurants in Hongdae, and sometimes in the evening they would even go to listen to hip-hop in night clubs.

It was around this time that Nabi learned that her grandmother was very ill. They had not seen each other for years. The old lady disapproved of the life her granddaughter had chosen, and whenever Nabi tried to get back in touch, she had been rejected coldly. Through a cousin, Nabi also learned with some satisfaction that there had finally been a scandalous incident. Pastor Randall had been unmasked after he assaulted a girl in the choir, and although in order to avoid a scandal, the parents (of course under pressure from the community) had not filed a complaint, the odious pastor had been sent very far away, to West Africa, or Vietnam, or somewhere else, and no one ever heard of him again. His wife with the large rump divorced him and found a new husband, so that order was fully restored. But Nabi felt a great bitterness at having been rejected and excluded, as if she had committed a fault. So when her grandmother left a message asking to see her again, Nabi did not hesitate. It was Namgil and Yumi who took charge of the meeting, and without consulting Nabi, managed to turn the reunion into a media event. It would take the form of a concert at the church. She was to sing hymns and spirituals in the presence of all the faithful, and under the eye of carefully selected cameras.

The ceremony took place one winter's evening, not long before Christmas. It had snowed, the fairy lights for the festival were already lit, and there were fir trees, gifts, and cotton balls hanging from plants inside the church, which was full to bursting. Nabi climbed onto the stage, where she had once appeared in her straight dress, or in denim jeans, and in sneakers. But for the night's ceremony, Namgil had prepared a red dress that clung close to her body and glittery shoes. In the first row, she noticed a free seat, and while she was wondering who was going to occupy it, she saw her grandmother arrive, supported by two women. The old lady was dressed in black, and her hair was tightly curled like a helmet. She was carefully made up to hide the pallor of her face. She walked slowly to her place, sat down, bolt straight, and looked at Nabi. It was a look of farewell, but the old lady showed no emotion. She did not smile, and her hard gaze drove into her granddaughter's eyes. Nabi sang as before, but almost without moving, her back well arched. First, she sang alone, then the musicians took up their guitars, the drummer began to beat the drums, and the audience came alive, singing together the words of the hymn, "Here I am to worship, here I am to bow down," clapping in cadence to accompany Nabi's songs, and at the end, after a long silence, their enthusiasm came flooding like a wave, when Nabi sang the words of "Arirang," slowly, in her grave, slightly husky voice.

That was all. There was no meeting. Namgil had been categorical.

"When you finish singing, you come down off

the stage and go straight out through the back door. Yumi will be there to help you."

He did not have to justify himself, for the last bars of the song were barely finished when the old lady rose from her seat, helped by the assistants, and headed for the back of the room without glancing backward.

"If she wants to see you again, Nabi, she'll know where to find you."

But apparently her grandmother had forgiven nothing, for the Christmas meeting ended without any follow-up. Towards the month of February, a message on her phone told Nabi of the death of her grandmother, after a stroke. She was astonished to find herself feeling nothing but a sort of echoing void, as if the celebration at the church had not finished resonating in her head.

It was during the same winter that Nabi learned that Yumi, whom she had considered her friend and called "Little Sister," had become Namgil's mistress. She also learned from her bank that her accounts had been emptied and that there was nothing left. The rent for the apartment in which she had been living had not been paid for more than six months, and the bank that owned it had begun eviction proceedings. At the end of the winter, in April, Nabi would have to leave. She had no place to go. She was terrified at the thought of having to change, to face reality. She had lived for the last five years as a kind of robot, between the noise of performances, the rehearsals with new musicians, and the silence of this apartment, waiting for the visits of Yumi, which had become increasingly rare, and now she understood why. As for Namgil, he had always been gentle and considerate, and they had even made love in the empty apartment, but then he left, always in a hurry, as if he were going to some business meeting, or returning home to his family. One day, he even presented himself to Nabi, displaying on his left cheek a long scratch, which he attributed to a wild cat, but Nabi understood that it was a mark Yumi had set on her lover's cheek so that everyone would know the truth. All this turned in her head, like a bad saw, producing the strident sounds of jealousy and contempt, which intoxicated her even more than the bottles of soju that she drank to fall asleep.

With the betrayal of Yumi and Namgil, Nabi's glory began to fade. The media had grown bored, they had found a younger girl, a rock singer, who wore mini shorts and lamé jackets, who dyed her hair red and was called Red-Haired Annie, after the animation. Silence entered Nabi's life. Now she hardly left the apartment, where she remained prostrate in front of the window, or dreamed that she was flying away, to the other side of the mountains, to the country where Mr. Cho and his mother had come from, a long time ago, and where he said he would return someday. Only the ex-policeman came, once a day, bringing her something to eat, nothing luxurious, just a part of his own lunch in a saucepan with a double bottom, rice with kimchi, marrow soup, a piece of salted hairtail. He understood that Nabi did not want to speak. He left the pan in front of the door, rang the bell, and left. Those were the only moments of humanity in her life.

It was the end of the story. Salome knew. Even if I wanted to keep going, I could not. She was leaning forward a little, the tendons of her neck protruding, and I saw at each side of her throat the pulsing of blood through her veins.

"Please go on, Bitna. Don't leave this story unfinished as you did before. I want to know everything about Nabi, I need to, you understand?"

It was not a matter of being paid. If I could, I would have given back all her 50,000 won bills and forgotten the grimacing smile of this lady in gold who had paid for my food and my rent in recent months. I wouldn't have hesitated.

"Please, please," Salome repeated in the weak, nasally voice of a capricious little girl. At the same time she swung around back and forth in an effort so difficult for her that the fingers clinging to the arms of her chair whitened.

I continued.

It was dawn when it happened. Dawn is the cruelest hour for those who suffer, because night gives way to the day, and they have not enjoyed any rest. Nabi walked to the small kitchen of the studio, or rather she slid across the floor, her legs bent under her. Maybe the alcohol and drugs made it hard for her to get up, or she did not want to see her reflection in the windows, in the mirror of the cupboard in the living room, on the screen of the television. In her hand, she held something she had never given thought to before, a metal hanger of the kind handed out at dry cleaners, with the neatly ironed dresses on them, buttoned up to the collar. Once on the floor of the kitchen, the hanger scraped along with an unpleasant sound. Maybe the neighbor below would once again complain. She herself is always complaining about the noises above her head, of high-heeled shoes, dishes rattling in the sink, or the feet of the sofa that wobbled when someone sits down too abruptly. Nabi tried to hold up the hanger, hook side up, but did not have enough strength in her arm, and the hanger clattered with even more noise. When a person dies, says the rumor, what they feel is not painful. On the contrary, it is as sweet as honey in the throat. It is intoxicating, like a perfumed smoke that fills the breast, and the door that opens up at the bottom of the brain is like the entrance to paradise. Then the soul escapes from the body through all the pores of the skin, through the eyes and ears, through the hair and through the nostrils, and scatters in the wind, travels over the waves of the sea, across the plains full of reeds and over the lotus leaves, amidst clouds as light as dragons, until it encounters a form with which it can unite, a living form, a blade of grass, a tree, a dragonfly, or a cat.

"Yes, I understand, it's the same cat who visited the hair salon, it's Kitty!"

Salome had become a little girl, again. Her face lit up with a smile. Maybe the pain had ceased for a moment in her body.

I did not know why, but her happiness pained me intensely. I stood up abruptly, to put an end to the idyllic lie.

"No, Salome, death is hideous."

When Mr. Cho finally entered the apartment a few days later, because the plates he placed in front of the closed door were still full and beginning to attract insects, he smelled the smell, and he understood. With his key card he opened the door, not without apprehension. But he had been a policeman, after all, and he continued to advance into the silent little apartment, until he saw Nabi hanging from the handle of the kitchen window, hanging by the neck by a simple twisted wire that was embedded in her flesh. Slowly, he unhooked the body, already cold and stiff, and laid it out on the tiled kitchen floor. He spoke in a low voice, as if afraid of waking Nabi. He simply whispered: "Why? Why?"

I left without saying goodbye, without greeting Mrs. Wang in the office. Soon, I would be liberated, I would no longer have to tell my stories. I would be able to begin to live for myself, in this great city, where all that mattered was the present and the world of the living.

A history of two dragons, for Salome

Late October 2016

"It's a story that's not really a story," I began.

Salome looked at me with her great feverish eyes.

I continued. "How can a story be told without really being a story?"

"If it's the truth," said Salome.

"Yes of course, but even the truth can be a lie if you do not believe it, and even a lie may seem true if I tell it well."

"So, what is it?"

"All right, I'll tell you. First, you have to know that the characters in this story do not exist."

"Because you invented them?"

I kept her waiting. I wanted her to understand that nothing is invented, even if nothing exists. I wanted it to be like a breath of air helping her live, for her who was so light, the air of a song without words, a breath of wind on her face between the window open on the street and the door of the office where Mrs. Wang was sitting.

"I told you, I never invent anything, which is why I called the two characters dragons, the Dragon of the

North, the Dragon of the South. They exist, you can be sure, but nobody can see them. I won't try to describe them, since they are invisible. They're like clouds, or like a reflection on the sea, or like the raindrops that you hear but cannot see."

"So how can I be sure they exist?"

"Because they are old, older than you and me. They have always existed, before this city, before this country, because you and I are just a moment in the history of the world, while they, these sleeping dragons, have been there from the beginning."

Salome closed her eyes, her head resting on the inclined back of the chair. Her hands lay flat on the armrests. She let herself sink into dreams, as if into sleep.

"Do you remember the story of little Naomi, the baby old Hana found on the steps of the Good Shepherd clinic?" I asked.

"Yes, I remember it. It was an unfinished story, right?"

"Not unfinished," I said. "It's still going on."

"Then tell me what happened to her, and what does she have to do with the two dragons?"

I hadn't realized before I began talking, but now everything seemed clearer. Each story was linked to the others, like people traveling in a subway car, not suspecting that they were destined to meet each another one day, somewhere in the great city of Seoul.

"As Naomi grew older, she became a very interesting little girl, maybe because she did not have her real parents."

"Like me," murmured Salome.

Naomi never called Hana her mother, even though she loved her very much. She seemed a normal child, sometimes with caprices and crises of despair, but her adoptive mother noticed little by little that she had a gift that the other children did not have. She saw things that no one around her saw. Old Hana had gone back to the maternity ward but finally stopped working there for good, because she was tired of the night service, and maybe because she was also afraid that they would not understand why she had kidnapped a baby.

So many of the babies arrived, in batches of ten or twelve, each month, and it was becoming difficult to find parents for them all, especially for those who were born with a disability, or blind from birth, or albinos, or with Down Syndrome.

Therefore, Naomi's disappearance had not aroused much anxiety. When the day nurses questioned her, Hana had lied with aplomb. She had been adopted by a family, of course. But when? Last week, by very good people, people in the government, they live on Namsan Mountain. They signed the papers, they even made a donation to the Good Shepherd. A gift? That had extinguished all suspicions. But when Hana left the orphanage, she changed her address, to make sure she was not asked any more questions.

To raise little Naomi, old Hana had resumed her former job as a cook in a small restaurant in the neighborhood, in the basement of a building, not far from Jongno. Naomi went to school in the neighborhood, and she had already learned to read and write, and to sing. She had a pretty voice when she sang children's songs, some in English. But the secret gift she possessed appeared one day as she was walking with her adoptive mother on a hill above Chungmuro. She pointed at a tree, a large tree, standing isolated at the foot of a rocky escarpment.

"There is a woman looking at us," she said.

Old Hana's eyes widened. "Well, I don't see

anything."

Naomi insisted. "Look, she's dressed in white, she's very beautiful." She smiled.

Hana had attributed this vision to the fantasy of an over-lonely little girl. She had not told anyone about it. To take her mind off it, she had registered Naomi for singing lessons after school. Once, as they were walking down the street after choir practice, Naomi had spoken of birds in the sky, many birds, flying in large circles, without crying, just the sound of their feathers in the wind. Yet, in the clear sky, there was nothing, not even a swallow, not even an airplane. Then Hana understood that Naomi was not like other children. She had received a gift to see the invisible.

Old Hana thought that if Naomi had this gift, she must know God. She took Naomi to the temple of Bongwonsa, a little way up a hill inside the city. It was a beautiful sunny day at the beginning of winter, and the trees were rust-hued. The taxi dropped them off at the entrance of the temple, and they started walking along the paths. In front of the sacred images, Hana prostrated herself several times, and Naomi imitated her. They lit incense sticks together and planted them in the large terracotta pot filled with white earth. Then they left, walking down the road as far as the bus stop to return to the Dongguk University neighborhood, where they lived.

"What did you see in the temple?" Hana asked a little later. She imagined that Naomi had received the blessing of Buddha, and that she had been transformed, transported with joy. But Naomi only complained of having sore feet.

"Maybe it's the wrong god," Hana thought. "Maybe she was born a Christian. After all, I know nothing about her family."

So Hana took her to Myeongdong Cathedral, a large brick building in the heart of downtown, in a bustling neighborhood, where it was surrounded by cinemas, pizza parlors, and cafés. But Naomi liked it no better. She even complained.

"It's dark in here!" she said. "Why does everyone look so sad?"

Old Hana was perplexed. If Naomi was not Buddhist or Christian, what was she?

One Saturday, as there was no school, Hana prepared an expedition. It was to the other end of the city, in the Ui-dong neighborhood, which was mostly small streets around a bus station.

In a kind of hangar, a tall woman, looking rather manly, was dancing on sword-blades. She was wearing several robes, which she removed one after another, turning upon herself. On her feet she wore large red-and-white American sneakers, and copper bracelets were clasped around her wrists. Some families had deposited offerings, bottles of alcohol, fruit, cigarettes, and money in half-open white envelopes. Hana also prepared some money, and she wanted to introduce her daughter so that she could receive the woman's blessing. But Naomi stayed behind. She did not want to show herself and hid her face in Hana's skirts.

"Don't be afraid. Give her your envelope!"

But Naomi refused to approach the woman. Her little hand held the crumpled envelope and refused to let go. The woman continued to turn on herself, and she stared at Naomi at every turn, with a look of anger, or perhaps of irony. Her mouth uttered incomprehensible words, sometimes in a deep voice, sometimes high-pitched. At the same time, she struck a small drum. Around her, the dresses she had thrown aside made fantastic shapes on the floor in the neon lighting. Then Hana understood that Naomi's attitude was disturbing the ceremony. The families had come to receive a blessing, so that their sons would succeed in the entrance exams for the national universities. They were looking askance at Hana and Naomi, afraid that everything would go wrong. So the old woman and the young girl fled with bowed heads, and in the subway ride back home, old Hana shifted guiltily under the black eyes of the little girl.

"Why did we go to see that nasty woman?" asked Naomi a little later.

Hana did not know how to answer.

It was around this time that Naomi started talking about dragons.

I paused, and Salome said in a dreamy voice, "I was born in the year of the dragon, did you know that?"

She had never told me her age, so I did a quick calculation.

"Does that mean you were born in 1976?"

"Yes, the first of February 1976."

That made her forty, or if calculated the Korean way, forty-one years old.

For the first time, I dared ask her, "Why did your

parents call you Salome? That means . . . bitch, doesn't it?" I used the English word "bitch," because it seemed to be the word that best captured the meaning.

Salome suddenly grew angry.

She answered in a flash, "No, I chose the name, because all I ever wanted to be was a woman who dances! Salome dances so well. But people are jealous of her fame. She's like little Nabi; people do not like others to be happy, they curse the girl who dances, and then one day she cuts off the head of John the Baptist!" It's a radical reversal.

Salome remained in a dreamy state. The afternoon was already well advanced, and the autumn light had taken on the color of the leaves of the ginkgoes in the avenue that ran along the side of the building. Maybe what Salome wanted to hear was a story of colors, a story of trees and mountains, so she could escape from the immobility of her apartment and breathe.

Naomi had a habit of looking up at the sky all the time. It was the only thing that interested her. Every day, she pulled old Hana by the hand, and they went out into the street. They walked towards Cheonggyecheon Stream, far from the apartment blocks.

"What do you see, Naomi?" Hana asked.

"What I see is not moving," Naomi said. "It's like two large snakes rolled together, and they're waiting."

"What are they waiting for?"

"They're waiting for their day to come," Naomi said simply.

Hana wondered what this day could mean. She looked up at the sky between the buildings, and she could see nothing, even when they walked as far as Samilgyo Bridge, and even when she squinted very hard.

One Sunday, they took the light blue subway line, got off at Chungmuro Station, and walked toward the mountain. Naomi squeezed Hana's hand.

"Here, I can see the dragons," she said. "They hide when there are too many people, too many cars."

Once they had walked as far as Namsan Library, a good distance from the subway, they sat on a stone bench, and Hana read aloud for Naomi an inscription on the library wall, a poem by the poet Yoon Dongju. Hana might have been inscribing the words into her own memory, as she remembered the war in which her grandfather had fought and died.

One star for memories and
One star for loving
One star for melancholia and
Another for longing
One star for poetry and
Another star for my mother

Naomi listened attentively, then said, "I like poetry when it talks about the stars."

After this, Naomi often talked about the two dragons. She didn't say what they looked like, or where they came from. She only said strange things, talking about "the day the dragons wake up," or saying, "When their moment comes, the dragons will unite."

As Naomi was still young, old Hana thought she was probably imagining things, so she bought her illustrated books about dragons. One day she told Naomi a story she heard when she was a child, about the Dragon of the Sea.

"Once upon a time, there was an old peasant woman who lived in the south, near a town called

Mokpo. She was alone in the world, because her husband and two sons had died in the war. She lived by making rice cakes that she sold at the Mokpo market every day. One day, as she was following the road to town, she met a tiger. The tiger was hungry, and he approached her to eat her, but she threw down a rice cake and ran away. Only she could not run very fast and already she felt the tiger on her heels, so she threw down a second cake, then a third, then another, but each time, the tiger would devour the cake and then resume his pursuit. Finally, the old peasant woman arrived on the beach. She had no more cakes to throw down, so she prayed to the Dragon of the Sea, 'Great Dragon, help me, please save me from this monster!' She had no sooner uttered this cry than the sea opened, and the Dragon of the Sea appeared. He told the peasant woman: 'Cross the sea with me. On the other side you will escape the tiger.' And that's what happened. The Dragon held back the sea and the old woman was able to pass to the island on the other side, and so she was saved."

Naomi asked, "What did this Dragon of the Sea look like? Tell me."

Hana did not know how to reply, and only said,

as Naomi had said, "He is just a Dragon, like those you see. Only that peasant woman has ever seen him, yet he exists, he sleeps in the sea."

Naomi did not ask any more questions. She knew that the two Dragons lived in the sky. She did not see them, she just felt their presence. It was like the breath of the hot wind in summer, or the whirlwinds that carry away the golden leaves of the ginkgoes.

"When their time comes," she said, "they will meet like two twin brothers who were separated at birth. The man who wrote the poems saw them, I am sure."

Old Hana did not doubt it either.

"It's always like that when there's a war or a calamity. The two Dragons move in their sleep, and when they wake up, it's Judgment Day."

Hana knew she was mixing everything up, the Bible, Buddha's commentaries, and even the boring stories that her grandmother had told her after the war.

The stalker appeared again.

I realized that he had probably never really let me go. He was an expert. A few drops of rain could hardly have discouraged him. I had underestimated him. I was in the subway when I recognized him. He looked different than he had when I was living in El Sordido. He appeared to be taller, dressed in an elegant suit, wearing fashionable black leather shoes, the toes a little too pointed. Instead of that ridiculous black woolen bonnet, which he had worn in summer, he was wearing a little blue-gray hat, like people who go to horse-races, or frequent the cafés of the expensive hotels in Jamsil.

It was at Jamsil that I saw him again. I had an appointment in an office building for an English translation, for a company. Insurers, or brokers, I was not very sure, I was replying to an ad on JobKorea. The pay was very reasonable, and it was the period before exams at school, so the Bitch had resumed her classes and no longer needed me. I had not been to visit Salome for two months, although I really needed the money to pay my rent. The meeting at Jamsil was scheduled for nine o'clock in the evening. The neighborhood was emptied of its office workers, and the large buildings looked like ocean liners, all their lights on but completely deserted.

I recognized the silhouette reflected in the subway window. He was a few rows behind me, and he was looking at me. I think it was his gaze that I first recognized. It pressed on my back, a little below my neck, and I had a feeling like cold water running down my spine. But we were on the subway, and there were people everywhere. People got on and off at each station. When my stop was announced, I decided not to move and waited to get off at the last moment, just before the doors closed. I had seen that in movies. It seemed like a good idea.

I walked quickly along the subway corridors, toward exit 4, which was close to the company's building. Despite the hubbub, I could hear the footsteps of the stalker behind me, far off. He was walking at the same pace as me, and the plastic heels of his new shoes echoed in the corridors, just like in the movies. I felt my heart beating at maximum speed. Despite the cold wind blowing in the corridors, I was sweating. Toward the end of the corridor, there was nobody else left, only me, and that noise pounding on the ground behind. I tried to think. If I started running, he would outrun me, and he would know that I knew he was there, and that I was afraid of him, that I was at his mercy. If I hid, in the shops selling umbrellas and belts, for example, he would know where I was, and wait until I came out. I wouldn't be able to hide forever in a shop three meters square, with an old woman asking me what I wanted to buy. I looked for a uniform, a police officer, a subway employee, or even a soldier, to ask for help, but you never see them when you need them. What if he had accomplices? Or suppose the next policeman I saw was just someone in disguise, who would grab me by the wrists when I approached him, and threaten me? I thought of who I could call, but no number came to my mind. I was really alone in the world. I even thought for a second of Salome, but it was stupid, what could a poor cripple do for me? I just thought of it for the story's sake, as if the denouement could be more important than the reality. She would say, "So what next?" And I would find an ending that would explain everything, an ending that would reassure, the final trick that would allow me to save myself, to stay alive. And quite curiously, this thought cured me of my fear.

Since I could imagine an ending, since I could see myself running, with the mechanical steps of this man in glossy black shoes, with his little maverick hat screwed onto his skull, it meant I was the master of the situation. I could change it, I could stop it, I could make it dissolve like a powerful image from a dream that evaporates minute by minute in the rays of the morning sun. That was it, I was living a dream. I was a character in a dream, and at the same time I saw myself acting, walking, swinging my arms, clasping my shoulder bag against my hip, turning my head slightly to catch the reflection of the stalker in a shop window. One two. One-two, one-two. I accelerated, one-two, one-two-three, like children who miss a step to walk faster, I even smiled at having such an idea.

When I arrived at exit 4, I hesitated. Suppose I went to the exit 6 instead and then crossed the avenue? I could run between the cars, profit from the chaos of the evening traffic on Jamsil to escape. But at the same time, I realized it was pointless. If it were not today, it would be tomorrow or the day after tomorrow. After all, I had moved as far as Oryu-dong, on the other side of town, and it had been pointless. I was sure he had followed me there, that he had passed under the bridge there, that he had seen me enter the building in front of the pork-meat restaurants and stayed down on the sidewalk until he saw the window in my room light up. He had lit a cigarette in contentment, he had smoked without moving. While I was thinking that I was far from him, that I had cut every tie, that I had escaped.

I now no longer felt fear but anger. That was what was making my heart beat and my chest swell. How could I have been so naive? Did I really know anything about life? Had I lived through all that, the wickedness of my cousin, the disdain of my aunt, the solitude, and especially the poverty, eating nothing but a little dry rice with stale kimchi, with nothing to drink but warm tap water, to end up the prey of a ferocious animal, perhaps wrapped in a black plastic bag, tied up, or cut into pieces, and thrown into the Hangang River? All these ideas were jostling in my head as I climbed the steps leading to the street, then walked along the sidewalk among the passersby, toward the large building lit up like a boat on the edge of a quay. Then I suddenly realized that the stalker was no longer following me. In the mirrors of the parked cars, in the shop windows, I no longer saw his figure. I could not hear the footsteps, because the uproar of the avenue was at its height, what with car engines, the high-pitched roar of buses rushing down the middle of the road, music from bars and shops selling phones or beauty products, and the loudspeakers, barkers and hustlers on every door step.

I crossed an alley, and a woman came toward me, dressed in white, rather like a nurse, or perhaps it was a wedding dress. She looked young, but as she approached I saw that she had a ravaged face. Her wrinkled, gray hair was tangled under a bonnet, and she wore a hygienic mask. When she arrived in front of me, she shouted something that I did not understand. I stood aside to let her pass. She looked at me and repeated what she had shouted.

"AIDS! AIDS!"

And she went walking on, with the passersby stepping out of her way as if she were stricken with the plague. Turning around, as if to follow her with my eyes, but using it as a pretext so that I could check that the stalker had really disappeared, I stopped to catch my breath, giving myself time to think. What if I had been deceived? Or maybe he had run into a policeman and was afraid I would report him? Or maybe today was not the right day. Like the dragons, maybe he was waiting for his day. He would only reveal himself at the right time. But when? When would he decide that it was the right day? Why tomorrow rather than now, why here at Jamsil, rather than at Oryu-dong, or on Salome's street?

The entrance to the building was right in front of me. I only had a few steps to go before I would be at the revolving door. But I was stopped. I did not understand at first, but then I saw a hand holding me by the shoulder, and an arm, strong and thick as a tree branch. I couldn't shout. I couldn't move. My legs trembled, my heart beat at full speed. I couldn't breathe. He was there, behind me, holding me back. His voice spoke in my ear, but I couldn't understand what he was saying. Quiet words, words whispered.

"Don't go in there. Don't go. It's a trap. Someone is waiting for you inside to hurt you."

There was nobody in front of the building, nobody on the other side of the door. The lobby was dark, and through the tinted glass of the door the ceiling lamps looked like four-ray stars. I could see the doors of the elevators. That was where I needed to go, and then up to the twelfth floor, that was where my meeting was.

Close to my ear, the voice repeated again, "Don't go in, it's a trap. If you go in there you risk losing your life."

I succeeded in freeing my arm and slipped out of the man's embrace. I pushed him away.

"Who are you? What do you want from me?"

He let go, taking two steps back. In the glare of the

streetlight, I couldn't see the features of his face, I only recognized his little plaid hat and his suit. He was not as tall as I had thought, and not as strong. I did not know if he was smiling, as he sometimes did. He smelled of cigarettes, alcohol. These were odors that reassured me.

"How do you know?" I asked him. I was no longer afraid of him. He was a man like any other. His little hat looked ridiculous. "Who are you, what is your name?"

He didn't answer right away. He kept repeating the same sentence.

"Do not go into the building. Someone is waiting for you. You are in serious danger."

I couldn't accept that. I shouted, "You are the danger. You have been following me for months. Who are you?"

He answered, as if it was completely normal, "It's my job to follow you. I was hired to protect you." And then he repeated his favorite phrase, with a more emphatic tone, as if he knew that I did not want to understand. "There is someone waiting for you in that building, someone who will hurt you, who will kill you."

Now I was very near the door. I looked at him again, and the empty, dark hall repelled me. I couldn't enter.

"Who paid you? Who asked you to protect me? I don't believe you."

Then I understood. The only person who could do that, the only one who knew everything about me, who had money and power, and also imagination, was the cripple in her chair, who had used Frederick Pak, who had organized everything, everything, from her yellow lounge at the far end of the city. It was so absurd that I could not help laughing, or rather, chuckling.

"Very well, go and tell her your story, tell her how you followed me on the subway and prevented me from going to my appointment, and how you saved my life!"

I turned away, without turning back. I walked along the broad avenue toward Jamsil Station, and without realizing it immediately, passed in front of the entrance to a church with a large double-winged door, closed now, and a neon sign. It was the kind of place where Nabi might have begun her career as a singer. It was when I had first arrived in this great metropolis, and when I began to go to the basement of the Jongno bookstore to flick through Japanese detective stories and especially the little novels of the Chinese writer Di An, who wrote for the naive provincial girls of all the countries in the world. Where I met Frederick Pak. I thought that Salome had no doubt engaged the stalker so that I could tell her about the fear I felt on being followed by a stranger. I thought to myself, now Salome would never know the end of the story of the would-be murderer, because her private detective, her guardian angel, had prevented me from entering the building where the murderer was waiting for me. Too bad for her!

After all these extraordinary events, I decided to move again. I was no longer afraid of the "stalker." I didn't know if he was still working as my guardian angel. Perhaps Salome had relieved him of his duties, because a watcher who has been identified is worthless. It was like a game, and in coming close to me, in warning me of the danger, he had broken the rules. I started receiving calls from Mr. Pak, alias Frederick, who proposed that we get together again. We met at the café Lavazza, where we used to meet, near Anguk Station. In that small neighborhood I found my new source of happiness, an independent room on the first floor of a small house whose owner was a Chinese *ajumma* named Mrs. Lu Lu, who lived with three cats. When I got back from classes in Hongik University, I sat in the café with a cappuccino, and while I waited for Mr. Pak, I wrote in a small notebook with white pages everything that came into my head. Songs, poems, even little axioms. I also wrote down my dreams.

From time to time Mr. Pak gave me news of Salome. Mr. Pak seemed to know her so well that I wondered if she had been his lover once, years ago, when he was still a schoolboy. That is what I imagined, but of course I could not discuss it with him.

"She is very low," he said. "She's fading away day by day. She's asking for you, and you refuse to take her calls."

What did that have to do with him. I was sarcastic.

"So you're her messenger now?"

He shrugged. "It's not like you to be nasty."

What did he know? To start with, one is not born wicked, one becomes wicked. This was one of the axioms I had written in my notebook.

I decided to resist, and not let myself be trapped by others. They all asked for something, they would not forget me.

Before I moved to my new place, I had been harassed every day by my aunt's calls. My cousin, the delicious Baekhwa, had run away. The whole family was in uproar. I absolutely had to do something, they told me. They feared for her life, or worse still, for her virtue! As if she had something to lose in that area. At first, I called back, explaining to my aunt that I had no idea what the girl was doing, or with whom, or where. It was not the right answer. My aunt insulted me, called me an egoist, a liar, a profiteer. After all she and her daughter had done for me, welcoming me when I came up to Seoul and knew nothing about the city. I was the daughter of Jeolla-do fishermen, capable only of skinning a hake. I hung up and did not take her calls anymore. There came a series of messages, some tearful, others threatening. I even feared that the fury would arrive in my home one day, that she would take the subway to Oryu-dong and then, with her customary cunning, obtain the keys and settle in my room, sitting on my bed, her legs wide open, her eyes smoldering. For that reason, I started looking for another place to live, as far away as possible from Oryu-dong, and I found it, thanks to a friend, at Mrs. Lu Lu's home in Insa-dong.

Then my aunt changed tactics. She got my mother to call me about Baekhwa. I talked with my mother about once a month, just a few words, to keep up to date, about the weather, work, money worries. I often thought of going back down to Jeolla-do, and sometimes felt bit nostalgic when I thought of the village, the street where nothing happens, just a few dogfights, and the drunks who fell flat in the sweet potato fields on Saturdays. But what I really missed was the sea. I liked to stroll on the harbor, in Mokpo, while my mother haggled with the fish merchants over hairtail and squid. I liked the smell of the sea, and the sound of the wind, and the lights of the fishing boats out on the open sea, like large motionless animals suspended in the night.

"Think of us, dear," my mother said. "She's the only daughter of your dad's sister. She's family, you can't ignore her."

To calm her down I said I'd take care of it.

"As soon as the exams are over, I'll have some free time."

I was lying. I knew I was not going to lift a finger to help Baekhwa. All my aunt needed to do was hire a private detective. If she wanted, I could give her the address of my stalker. I don't remember anymore what else I said to my mother then, and if she repeated it to my aunt, but it set a great gulf between us, and I had some peace. Then, a while after, I heard that Baekhwa had come home. Her father slapped her, her mother scolded her, and then they forgave her, and everything was back in its proper order. That is how we make delinquents and lost girls. Another axiom.

Now I am beginning to understand what has happened in my life, since I first met Salome. I never thought about it before. It is all so strange, almost incredible. I don't know if it was a coincidence, or if it was a kind of waking dream. When I think of it, it seems to me that everything was arranged in order to bring about our story, that I have been in some way the messenger of a superior, heavenly order, and that I shall never be the same person again. So here is my last story, that I shall tell Salome before it is too late. It is for her that I want to invent it, to explain to her that she is the only person who has ever counted in my life, more than my own parents, more than Frederick, the only person among the millions and millions of human beings that exist in this city of Seoul, in all its neighborhoods, all its buildings, streets and roads, bridges and subway tunnels, and even in its great Hangang River, which has seen all wars, crimes, and passions unfold on its banks. And its green and yellow water keeps on flowing, down to the sea, where it mingles with the dirty waters of the ocean, never to return.

Crossing the rainbow bridge, for Salome
April 2017

This is a true story, my only true story. I do not mean to say that the other stories I told Salome to cure her of her pain were false, but I arranged them to please her. I added sweet little words, harsh little words, so that she could understand what was happening in the world she did not know, the world where people move, feel the warmth of the sun, the chill of the winter winds, the rain, the snow. The world that is cruel and selfish, because it does not bother about her. The world that will not miss her when she dies.

Early one Sunday morning, little Naomi came down from her mother's apartment on the twelfth floor. In front of the building stretched a small, narrow garden. In the snow, at the foot of a tree, a magnolia that did not lose its leaves in winter, Naomi saw a little ball of brown feathers, motion-less, shivering, a bird that seemed to be asleep. As she drew close, the bird opened its beak and cried. "*Ppyak-ppyak!*"

Naomi crouched down to look at it and asked, "Well, what's the matter with you? Are you lost?"

It replied with the same shrill cry, "*Ppyak-ppyak!*" At the same time, it beat its wings and shook the feathers of its neck, which became all ruffled up. Naomi stayed motionless for a moment, and when she started to move away, the bird rose to follow her. It took refuge between her feet, lifted its head, shook its wings, and kept repeating its cry, "*Ppyak!*" as if to say, "Take me with you!" Naomi thought that if she left it there, the neighborhood cats would soon make a mouthful of it, so she picked it up. It submitted, its little claws clinging to Naomi's fingers as if they were branches, its nails digging into her skin.

Naomi went back up to the apartment, and as her mother was not there, and she did not know where to put the bird, she put it on a towel in the sink. She gave it a drink of water, first in a mug, but it did not know what to do with that, then in the hollow of her hand, and it drank all the water. It must have fallen from the tree long before and not drunk or eaten anything since. In the warmth of the apartment, it seemed more alive. It shook its feathers, beat its wings, and Naomi saw that the feathers of the wings were a wonderful color, a bright blue, with a few black feathers along the edges. It was surely the most beautiful thing Naomi had ever seen. She waited for her mom to come back.

When old Hana saw the bird, she exclaimed, "It's a jay, that bird of yours, a jay from the forest, it's called an *eochi.*"

So that was the name Naomi gave it. O'Jay, as if it were Irish. Hana said it would probably die, because little birds that fell from their nests no longer had their mothers to feed them.

"What does O'Jay eat?"

Hana said it ate everything, especially the insects and caterpillars it found on trees in the forest. Fortunately, old Hana was a daughter of the sea, and she knew where to find worms for fishing. She took Naomi to the market in Namdaemun, near the station, where there were small stalls selling bait for people going fishing, and they bought a bag of maggots.

Naomi fed O'Jay his first meal with wooden chopsticks. She held the maggot in front of his beak, and he swallowed it. Then he shook himself contentedly and opened his beak wide, uttering his shrill cry of "*Ppyak!*" to ask for another maggot. The whole of the following week was a delight for Naomi and for old Hana. They took turns feeding O'Jay. They talked to him. They cleaned up his droppings. Naomi realized that O'Jay liked to leave his droppings on paper, and old Hana went looking for old newspapers, even used books. At first, she tried to get O'Jay to sleep in a cage, but he didn't want to. As soon as he was shut in, he would utter his most desperate "*Ppyak!*" and Naomi would take him into her hands. He never left her. Everywhere she went, O'Jay followed her, even to the bathroom and to the toilet. Hana explained, "You're the first person he saw when he fell from his nest, so he thinks you're his mom."

When Hana left for work, she left O'Jay on a tree branch she had picked up in the garden of the building and attached to the sink with sticky paper. And when Naomi came back from school, she rushed into the apartment with her heart beating, and O'Jay welcomed her with his shrill cry, as if to say, "Mamma, I'm hungry!" and beat his wonderful blue wings. Naomi gave him some maggots to eat, made him drink water from her hand, then lay down on the floor and put O'Jay on her chest to warm him.

"Listen to my heart," she said.

She knew that babies liked nothing better than to hear the beating of their mother's heart, and since O'Jay had decided she was his mom, he needed to be reassured.

Salome's hospital room is the exact opposite of her apartment. It's all white. The window is a square of raw light that the plastic blinds hardly filter. Salome lies on the bed, the top of her body enclosed in a kind of iron cylinder that pumps in, then out. I can see only her thin legs, her feet and arms, and her emaciated face. Around her eyes, the skin is gray, and her hair is held back by clips. But she still has the ordinary face of Rossetti's Sister Swallow. With her eyes closed, her mouth, made thin by illness, fixed in a kind of pale smile, she also looks like the Ophelia painted by John Everett Millais, a picture I loved so much when I was twelve that I pasted it on the wall of my room in Jeollado. When I begin to talk about Naomi, Salome's eyelids tremble a little, as if to signal to me that she is listening, that she has been waiting for me. Frederick warned me, "If you do not go now, it will be too late."

That is not what made me decide to come. It was the memory of a bird I cared for when I was a child, that escaped from me little by little. I wanted to share that bird with Salome. Not that she is as dear to me as that animal I cared for until the end, but because this history is common to all living creatures. Together with the moment of birth, it is the most mysterious story of our lives.

For a few weeks, Naomi lived a love story with O'Jay. When she came back from school, she would go rushing into the bathroom, and the blue bird welcomed her with his little cries. They weren't just cries of hunger, they were also cries of happiness at seeing her again after a very long absence in the darkness of the little room. Naomi took him and put him on her shoulder, where he would peck at her ear with his beak, and nibble her hair. Then began the feeding session, the mealworms and the maggots that Naomi gave him by the beakful at the tip of wooden chopsticks. To make him open his mouth she would say: "Ah, ah," like any mother holding out a spoonful of food to her child. Yet something was wrong, Naomi realized. There was a small white ball at the base of his beak. She talked about it with Hana, and they decided to take O'Jay to Seoul National University, to the College of Veterinary Medicine. It was Yujin, a friend of Hana who worked in the maintenance services there, who made the appointment. The diagnosis was cruel. O'Jay was infected with a virus that killed wild birds, deforming their beaks and clogging their trachea. He was doomed, and the veterinarian proposed an immediate euthanasia, to avoid suffering and to prevent contagion of other wild birds.

Naomi returned home in tears. She had not agreed to have him put down, despite Hana's reasonable words.

"You have to accept it, Naomi, it's the only solution for him, and for you too. You can't prevent what is bound to happen."

But how could she give up O'Jay now? He loved her and put all his trust in her, he followed her everywhere, ate so well, and then after eating sang and stretched his wings to show off his blue feathers. She who had never prayed would pray, she would ask all the saints and spirits she had met in her dreams to help poor O'Jay to recover.

From that day on, each moment of O'Jay's life was one that delayed destiny, it was one day, one hour gained against the disease. Each beakful eaten gave him strength, and every heartbeat of Naomi made his heart beat in his breast, that little heart she felt through the down when she held him in her hands. To distract O'Jay, Naomi bought a CD with recordings of birdsong, and she played it on Hana's computer. She searched for recordings of mountain jays on the internet and made him listen. O'Jay opened his eyes wide and seemed to like that music. Then, at night, he fell asleep snuggled against her, and before she went to sleep, Naomi would put him on the branch, so she could listen, ready to act if something happened. At night, she did not sleep, she thought of everything O'Jay would be able to experience if he lived, the taste of the wind in the sky, the green carpet of the rice fields below him, the mountains and the forests, the smell of pines in the sunlight when he hunted for worms in their bark, as Naomi had taught him.

"Don't die, please," Naomi murmured, as in prayer. "You have so many beautiful things to see in the world. You escaped from danger and I saved you. Don't die!"

Salome is listening to the words of my story. I know she loves it because sometimes her eyelids open, and a tear shines in her black eyes. I sit down on the iron chair next to the bed.

A doctor, a woman of Salome's age, who perhaps feels sorry for this woman at the end of her illness, says to me, "She doesn't seem to be aware of anything, because of the medicine she is being given to lighten her pain. But talk to her, she will hear you. Even if you think she is asleep, she will hear you."

I am the only person who visits her every day, perhaps because I don't have any work, and exams are over. I didn't pass. I've probably lost a year, and it's possible that I won't be able to afford to continue and will have to go back south, far from Seoul, to help my mother in her work. Mr. Pak, Frederick, that lover of Chopin, told me that he is leaving soon for the States. He's been accepted into a great university, Rutgers (pronounced "Ruckers," I don't know why). He didn't suggest that I join him, and anyway, could I really do that? Salome is outside of all these things. She is on an island, far from noises and storms, and my voice is the only thread that holds her.

O'Jay was losing his strength. At first, he had rushed at food as soon as the wooden chopsticks were held out, but now he turned his head away. From time to time, he uttered his cry, that sharp "*Ppyak,*" but Naomi could hear that there was no longer any joy in his call, but rather something like anger and fear, an unanswerable question. To distract him, she would hold him close to her and they would go walking together in front of the building, in the bare little garden, between the trees. Naomi thought he might recognize the place where he was born, or remember his mother, his nest. But O'Jay trembled as soon as they were outside. He closed his eyes and pressed against the little girl's neck. The world was too big, the sky too white, the cold wind penetrated his down, and he did not have the strength to cling to the branches that Naomi held out. Or perhaps he feared that the little girl might abandon him in a tree. There was nothing to be done, as the veterinarian had told her. "Sooner or later, you will have to bring him to me, so that we can help him die. He will ask you to do it himself, and if you love him you will have to do him that service."

Old Hana said nothing, but she watched Naomi

when she held the bird tight against her chest, and she sighed. Love is an ordeal, she thought. She had felt all of this when she had taken Naomi away from the orphanage. It was a commitment that could not be betrayed. Once you had begun you had to go on until the very end.

At night, now, Naomi no longer put O'Jay on the branch. She kept him with her on her breast (with a cloth to hold the droppings) until he fell asleep. Then, very gently, she placed him on his perch, for fear of hurting him while she slept. She listened to him breathing. She had never thought that such a small animal could make a noise when it breathed, with a little cry from time to time, as if dreaming, a very gentle hiss. Every minute of his sleep was precious to Naomi. She too fell asleep, a light sleep, peopled with strange dreams. She dreamed of all the creatures she had seen since her childhood, some very sweet, others baleful, frightening. She often dreamed of the two dragons in the Seoul sky, covering the city and the river, and sometimes moving slowly, one against the other. She dreamed that she was flying away with O'Jay. Together they roamed above the countryside, over the forests and rice paddies, as far as the islands out in the sea.

Salome wants to move, too. Perhaps the pressure sores on her back are causing her pain, or she feels cramps in her legs. I massage them gently, as I learned to do for my grandmother. I press on the hardened tendons, on the muscles, and with my fingers I urge the blood and lymph upward, very slowly. The respirator makes a sound like surf on the pebbles of a beach, and the cardiac monitor emits shrill whistles. The nurse needs to come soon. She comes, the pale one, with long black hair fixed in a bun beneath her bonnet. She pushes a syringe into the tube connected to the vein on Salome's right hand, injecting a cloudy liquid that takes away the pain.

"She's going to sleep now, until tomorrow morning."

The nurse closes the blinds, and darkness invades the room, but the corridors remain illuminated by neon tubes. I get up and walk noiselessly to the door.

That night, Naomi was awakened by a noise. She got up at once, and she saw that O'Jay had fallen from his perch and was lying on the white towel. Naomi took him up delicately in her hands, and placed him against her heart, whispering soft words, but O'Jay remained inert, his head thrown back. Then Naomi remembered the first aid lessons at school. She blew into his slightly opened beak, so that he would start breathing again.

"Wake up O'Jay, I beg you."

After a moment, O'Jay awoke. His eyes opened halfway, they looked up at Naomi, but his gaze was vague, far off. She felt him tremble, his wings tried to open again and show the feathers that were so blue, to please the little girl.

He cried twice, "*Ppyak-ppyak.*"

He would have liked to have given a joyful cry, but he instead gave a cry of suffering, because the life was seeping away from his body and he was trying in vain to retain it.

"O'Jay ... O'Jay ..."

Naomi whispered. She breathed again into his mouth, she massaged his heart through the down. The bird stiffened once, head back, as if trying to fly. His wings were open in Naomi's hands. He was dead.

Now Salome can no longer hear. She has been in a coma since the day before. The respirator continues to sound like the sea, breathing in, breathing out, making its cruel noise. She does not cry out, nor breathe a word when the life leaves her body. She just suddenly turns very white. I try to save her. I massage her legs and arms, I blow on her lips. She is already far away, setting off across the rainbow bridge, like O'Jay. Her body remains on the hospital bed, her chest attached to the breathing machine, her wrists bound to the tubes that send their clouds of milky forgetfulness into her veins. I had thought that her death would not affect me, on the contrary that it would relieve me, since it released me from her grasp, from her malice. Then suddenly my feelings of rancor ceased, almost like the octopuses that my father turns over when they have just been caught, back home in Jeolla. Salome had been the only person who really cared about me in all this vast city of Seoul, where nobody ever meets anyone. She wanted me to live for her, to tell her about life outside. Certainly she used me, but she also protected me. So my eyes were full of tears when I had to leave her.

Naomi spent the whole night beside O'Jay. In the morning, before her mother was awake, she went down to the garden of the building. She dug with her bare hands a grave in the ground at the foot of the magnolia, and deposited O'Jay's body in it, laying him on his side, with his head back like when he used to wait for food. She did not plant any flowers. She did not say any prayers. The whole world was asleep. Even the two dragons in the sky of Seoul were still asleep, intertwined with one another. She shed tears. She would never be the same again. For now she knew how hard it was to die, when all the body and all the mind wanted to go on living, and how all that could be done was cry, tremble and stiffen, before your spirit flew across the bridge of wonderful colors.

She never forgot him. Every day, before going to school, or after returning home, she stopped in front of the magnolia and talked to O'Jay. She told him about her day, what funny or sad things she saw, the weather, the sun and the wind, the flowers that would open, and even the little worms that moved inside the trees, as if saying, "Eat us, eat us." And sometimes she heard a sound of wings in the sky, and shrill cries, and she knew that O'Jay was not far away, that he would come back soon.

I am Bitna, and I am nineteen. I'm alone in this great city of Seoul, alone under the sky. I have known many people, many adventures, some which have been told to me, others that have been birthed in my dreams, or in my life. I did not go to the funeral of Salome, or Kim Seri. I am not sure if Mr. Frederick Pak was there. Salome's family did not like him. They said (and he himself told me, one day when he wanted to tell me more about himself) that he was a *jebi*, a swallow, a bird dressed in black and white that takes advantage of others and steals everything that can be stolen. A gigolo. I think they're not so wrong. He is a man like many men. He takes what he wants, then leaves without looking back.

I walk beneath the sky of Seoul. The clouds slowly roll by. Over Gangnam it is raining. Toward Incheon the sun sets, kindling a bright glow, and Bukhansan Mountain emerges from the rain to the north, towering like a giant. I am alone. My life is about to begin.

Seoul–Paris–Seoul
April–September 2017